"Tell Me Why You're Le

He couldn't seem to help himself, and lifted his finger to trace her lips. Her breath caught, and his face darkened as he watched.

Kiss him, tell him it's him and that he's going to be a father!

But while all these impulses rampaged through her, she drew back an inch, considering it a good moment to retreat before she truly lost her senses. She'd lost them once. Now she was pregnant. She didn't want to castigate him for that night, a night she had been wishing and praying someday happened. But she didn't want him to pay his whole life.

She simply loved him too much.

* * *

If you're on Twitter,
tell us what you think of Harlequin Desire!
#harlequindesire

Dear Reader,

I've wanted to write Garrett and Kate's book ever since I wrote *Paper Marriage Proposition* and I got to meet them. I could feel their chemistry leap off the pages, and it wasn't even their book yet. In Julian and Molly's story, *Wrong Brother, Right Kiss,* you get to meet them, too, and once more I couldn't wait to write their love story.

Once Pregnant, Twice Shy wasn't an easy story to write. It turns out they both want each other, but they've spent years denying themselves—it was really hard to get them to finally drop their walls. They needed time and little sparks of realization to really realize what they had going on between them. I guess it's not easy to reel a man like Garrett Gage in, but when you do, he's all in. I hope you enjoy their story like I did!

With love,

Red

ONCE PREGNANT, TWICE SHY

RED GARNIER

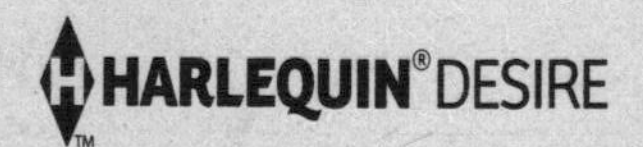

ISBN-13: 978-0-373-73311-8

ONCE PREGNANT, TWICE SHY

This edition published by arrangement with Harlequin Books S.A.

For questions and comments about the quality of this book, please contact us at CustomerService@Harlequin.com.

Printed in U.S.A.

Books by Red Garnier

Harlequin Desire

Wrong Man, Right Kiss #2248
Once Pregnant, Twice Shy #2298

Silhouette Desire

The Secretary's Bossman Bargain #2028
Paper Marriage Proposition #2064

RED GARNIER

is a fan of books, chocolate and happily ever afters. What better way to spend the day than combining all three? Traveling frequently between the United States and Mexico, Red likes to call Texas home. She'd love to hear from her readers at redgarnier@gmail.com. For more on upcoming books and current contests, please visit her website, www.redgarnier.com.

As always, with my deepest thanks to everyone at Harlequin Desire—who make the best team of editors I've ever come across! Thank you for making this book shine.

This book is once again dedicated to my flesh-and-blood hero and our two little ones, who, it turns out, are not so little anymore.

Prologue

He was the sexiest best man the maid of honor had ever seen, and he wouldn't stop looking at her.

Stomach clenched tight with longing, she stared into his gorgeous obsidian eyes and wondered how she was going to have the courage to tell him that their one incredible night together, that night that should have never happened but *did,* had resulted in a little surprise on the way.

That the stork would be paying them a visit in eight months or so.

The thought alone made her legs tremble. Clutching her white orchid bouquet with trembling hands, Kate Devaney forced herself to focus on her sister, Molly, and how stunning she looked up on the altar in her snow-white wedding gown next to the drop-dead-gorgeous groom.

The fresh noon sun lit her lovely pink-cheeked face, its warm rays illuminating the couple as they stood before the priest. They were surrounded by an explosion of white casablancas, orchids, tulips and roses. The train of the bride's wedding gown reached almost to the end of the red velvet carpet, where the guests sat in rapt attention on rows and rows of elegant white benches. Molly's voice trembled with emotion as she spoke her vows to Julian, her best friend for forever, and the man she'd always loved.

"I, Molly, take you, Julian John, to be my husband…"

Kate's heart constricted with emotion for her little sister, but no matter how much she fought the impulse, her eyes kept straying to the right side of the groom…to where the best man stood towering and silent.

Garrett Gage.

Her tummy quivered when their eyes met again. His eyes were hot and tumultuous, his jaw set tight and square as a cutting board.

He'd been looking at her for every second of the ceremony, his palpable gaze boring pinprick holes through the top of her head.

What a pity that his fiancée wasn't at the wedding, so that he could go and stare at that blonde and leave Kate alone, she thought angrily.

But no, he haunted her. This man. Day and night she thought of him, wanted him, ached for him, while every second of the day, she tried futilely to forget him.

For the past month, it had been a struggle to ignore the enticing memories of the things he'd said to her, a struggle not to remember the way he'd held her in his strong, hard arms like she was more precious than platinum.

She'd told herself, every night for the past thirty nights, that they would never work, and when she'd finally heard of his upcoming marriage, she'd had no other choice but to believe herself.

It was fine. Really. She hadn't wanted to marry him. She would never marry unless she could have what Molly and Julian had; if Kate couldn't have a little piece of real love for herself, then she'd rather be alone.

So tomorrow she was leaving. She had a one-way ticket to Florida. Miami, to be precise. Where she could begin a new life and never have to see the man she loved with another woman again. But before she left, she must let him know the truth. A truth she had been carefully keeping to herself for a month, not wanting to detract from the joy of Molly's big day.

Molly was her only sister; Kate had practically raised her since they had both been orphaned as little girls. She wanted Molly's wedding day to be perfect.

Yes, Kate was pregnant, but there was still plenty of time to find the right moment to tell Garrett about it. If only he'd stop looking at her like he wanted her for lunch, making her insides twist and clench with yearning.

"You may now kiss the bride!"

Startled, Kate couldn't believe she'd missed so much of the ceremony, and then she watched as the handsome, blond-haired Julian lifted Molly in his arms as if she weighed no more than a feather and kissed the breath out of her.

Arms twining around him, Molly squeaked in delight as Julian swung her full circle, still kissing her. But he pulled back with a frown and murmured, "Oh, crap!" when he realized Molly's train had gone round and round both their bodies.

When they looked down to the coil around them, they both burst out laughing, then they started kissing again, Julian's open hands almost engulfing all of Molly's petite face as he cradled it.

"I got it," Kate said, laughing as she easily detached the train from her sister's dress. With Molly in his arms, Julian hopped out of the tulle and carried her down the aisle to the cheers and claps of their guests and the blaring sound of the "Wedding March."

They looked so happy, so in love, as they headed for the beautifully decorated gardens where their outdoor wedding celebration was to take place, leaving Kate behind with a pair of stinging eyes, the train and the best man.

As Kate began gathering what felt like a hundred miles of tulle, Garrett came over, bringing her the other end of the train. She couldn't seem to look up at him. "Thanks," she said, and felt her cheeks burn. God, why was she even blushing? They'd grown up together. He should be a man she was comfortable with and instead she was a wreck just wondering how she was going to tell him.

Despite how much it hurt her to know he was marrying someone else, she didn't want to ruin his life, because he'd always protected and cared for her. Always.

And she feared this news was going to be a whopper for him.

Suddenly his tan, long-fingered hands captured and stilled hers, and she held her breath as the warmth of his palms seeped into her skin. She looked up and into those riveting onyx eyes, her lungs straining for air.

"Tell me if I'm mistaken—" his voice was low, his eyes so unbearably intimate she could die "—but did my brother just marry your sister?"

She wouldn't stare at his beautifully shaped lips as he spoke. She wouldn't. But, oh, God, he was so handsome she could burst from it. "It only took a full hour, Garrett. You couldn't have missed it," she said, trying to keep her voice level.

And yet, maybe she was hallucinating, but…was he staring at *her* lips? "Apparently I did."

"You were standing right there. Where were you? Mars?" She straightened and rolled her eyes, ready to leave, but his voice, the intensity in his words, stopped her.

"I was in my bedroom, Kate. With you in my arms."

She went utterly still, her back to him, while every inch of her body fought to suppress a tremor of heat that fluttered enticingly down her spine. His words seduced her body and soul in ways she couldn't even believe were possible. Her legs felt watery, and every pore in her body quivered with wanting of him. His words transported her to his bedroom. To his arms. To that night.

No, no, no, she couldn't do this here. She just couldn't.

Shaking her head almost to herself, she started down the beautiful red path that led to the Gage mansion, painfully aware that he followed.

"Kay, I need to talk to you," he said thickly.

That low, coarse timbre managed to do sexy things to her skin, and her physical response to him irritated her beyond measure.

"If it's to tell me about your wedding, I already know. Congratulations," she said in a voice as flat as the bottom of her shoe.

"Then maybe you can tell me the details, since apparently you know more about it than I do? Dammit, I need to talk to you somewhere *private*."

He grabbed her elbow to halt her, but she immediately yanked it free. "I need to talk to you, too, but I'm not doing it here. Nor am I doing it *today*."

He followed her again with long, easy strides, the determination in his voice nearly undoing her. "Well, I *am*. So just listen to me." He stopped her again, forced her to turn and stared heatedly into her eyes. "I don't know what happened to me the other day, Katie.... What you told me left me so damn winded, I swear I didn't know where to begin...."

She covered her ears. "Not here, please, *please not here!*"

He seized her wrists and forced her hands down. "I know I hurt you, I know you don't want me to apologize, but I need to say I am sorry. I am sorry for how things have gone down and for hurting you. I'm sorry how it happened, Katie. I wish I'd done it differently. If I could take it back, I would, if only to get you to stop looking at me like you are just now."

His apology was the last straw. It really was. The last. Straw. "You wish to take the night back, that's what you wish?" The pitch of her voice was rising, but she couldn't control the hysteria bubbling up inside her chest, couldn't stop herself from incredulously thinking, *How can I take back the baby you gave me, you ass!* "Oh, you're something special, do you know that? You're something else. I can't even believe I let you put your filthy paws on me, you no-good—"

"Goddammit, I really didn't want to do it this way, Kay. But you're giving me no choice!" Teeth gritted, he scooped her up into his arms and stalked across the gardens toward the house.

"Wha—" The tulle train fell inch by inch from her grasp and trailed a path behind them as she kicked and squirmed and hit his chest. "Garrett, stop! Put me down! What are you *doing?*"

He kicked the front doors open and carried her up the stairs, his jaw like steel, his hands blatantly gripping her buttocks. "Something I should've done a long, long time ago."

One

Two months earlier...

This was hell.

The Gage family mansion was lit up with light and music and flowers tonight. All the movers and shakers in San Antonio seemed to be having a good time, a good wine and a good laugh. But Kate had gone well past purgatory an hour ago and was now sure that this night, this endless night, was nothing other than hell.

With a sinking feeling in the pit of her stomach, she watched the striking couple across the glittering marble floor.

"Garrett," the slight, sensual blonde gushed to the tall dark man, "you're just like fine wine, better and better with age."

Garrett Gage, the sexiest man on the planet, and the

devil in Kate's hell, ducked his head and whispered something into the woman's ear with a wicked gleam in his dark eyes.

How many nights had she dreamed Garrett would look at her like that? Not like a little girl, but like a woman?

In a black suit and blood-red tie, with his dark hair slicked back to reveal his chiseled features, standing proud and imposing like the media baron he'd become, Garrett Gage could cause lightning to strike. He could make butterflies rise in your stomach. Make the earth stop. Make your heart thump. He could make you do *anything* just for a chance to be the one woman at his side.

For years, Kate had thought that feeding him, seeing him enjoy and praise her creations, was good enough. The next best thing to having sex with him, she supposed. But now it just pained her to cook and cater for a man who didn't even notice that *she,* Kate Devaney, the woman who made the chocolate croissants he so loved, was on the menu, too.

If only one of her waiters hadn't failed her at the party tonight, Kate might have showcased her new dress with just the right amount of hip sway to finally draw Garrett's discerning eye. But with a tray fixed permanently to her shoulder, no one spared a glance at the glossy satin dress she wore; she was just passing the food.

"Darling, be a dear and bring over some of those cute little shrimp skewers with the pineapple tips," a woman said as she swept up a crab-and-spinach roll and guided it to her lips.

"Orange-pineapple shrimp? It'll be right over," Kate said.

Grateful for the distraction, she swept back into the kitchen to load up a new tray. Usually the sight of her workers milling about the three-tiered cake and pulling out mouthwatering snacks and hors d'oeuvres from the oven would fill her with satisfaction. But even that didn't lift her spirits tonight. *Eight more weeks, Kate. Just two months. And then you never have to see him with another woman again.*

As she carried a new tray into the busy living room, it struck her that she was going to leave behind this house with so many good memories, and this family who'd practically raised her as one of their own. She'd been so happy here; she'd honestly never imagined leaving until her feelings for Garrett had become so…painful. Moving to Florida was the best thing to do—the healthiest. For her. To be away from that hardheaded *idiot!*

"Mother tells me you're leaving." Julian John fell into step beside her as she navigated past a large group. Kate had been so deep in thought that she started at the low, sensual voice.

She glanced up and into the gold-green eyes of the youngest Gage brother, a beautiful man with a heartbreaking smile who was known to be guarded and quiet—except with Molly. He was only two months away from marrying Kate's perky and passionate younger sister and officially becoming her brother-in-law. But if Julian already knew about her departure—*who else did?* Her stomach cramped in dread.

"I can't believe she's told you. I asked her not to tell."

Julian plucked a shrimp skewer from the tray and popped it into his mouth. Like all Gage men, he had massively broad shoulders, and his symmetrical, masculine face looked as if it had been cast in bronze. "Knowing my mother, she probably thought you meant not to tell the press—and that would exclude its owners."

Kate smiled. At seventy, still stout and active, the Gage matron was a force to be reckoned with. She was the proud mother of three strong, successful media magnates—not that Landon, Garrett and Julian John were powerful enough to keep the sassy woman from having her say.

She glittered tonight in a high-end ruby-colored dress, which was completely undermined by the plain black bed slippers she wore. Comfort, to her, was everything. She didn't care what others thought and had enough money to ensure that everyone would at least *pretend* they thought the best of her.

She'd been the closest thing to a mother to Kate, who'd grown up without one. At the tender age of seven, she and her bodyguard dad had moved in to this very house where Garrett's birthday celebration was being held. Her father had died shortly after, leaving Kate and Molly orphans, but this house had remained their home.

"Nothing Molly and I can do to change your mind?" Julian asked, gold-green eyes flicking across the room toward Molly.

Kate could melt when she saw the glimmer of pride and satisfaction in his eyes when he looked at her sister.

It only reminded her of what she herself wanted in her future.

A family of her own.

Which was why she had to leave and rebuild her life, find other interests, and find herself an actual love life with a man who *wanted* her.

"I really have to do this, Jules," she told him as she shook her head and extended the tray to the people standing opposite him. Within seconds, the shrimp skewers started to disappear, one by one.

She had to get away, before she ended up watching the man she loved marry another, form a family. Before she became the dreaded "Aunt Kate" to children she'd always wished would be hers.

"But don't tell Garrett yet, okay? I don't want him on my back already."

"Hell, nobody wants that man on their back. Of course I won't tell him."

Smiling at that, she stole a glance in his direction, and yes, he was still there, as gorgeous as he'd been a minute ago, the blonde looking completely absorbed in him.

The woman was some sort of business associate of his who clearly enjoyed raising men's temperatures. Kate didn't know her, but already she abhorred her.

Seeming distracted, Garrett glanced around the room, and his liquid coal eyes stopped on Kate. Her heart stuttered when his gaze seemed to trail down the length of her silky form-fitting dress—the first male eyes to take in her attire tonight—then came back up to meet her startled stare.

Suddenly the look in his eyes was so dark and unfathomable, she almost thought that he—

No.

Whatever emotion lurked in his eyes, it was swiftly concealed. He raised his wineglass in the air in a mock toast, and added a smile that, although brief and friendly, went straight to her toes.

But that smile had nothing on the one he gave his companion when he turned away from Kate. His lips curled wide, with a flash of white teeth, and Kate just knew the poor woman was done for.

So was Kate.

Damn it, why hadn't she gotten one of those wolfish smiles?

Garrett had been there for her for as long as she could remember. A permanent fixture in her life. Steady and strong as a mountain. Her father had died for him. And Garrett had taken the promise he'd made to the dying man to heart.

Now Garrett protected Kate from raindrops and hail, from snow and heat, from kittens with claws and barking dogs. He even protected her from bankruptcy by ensuring the family always had a catering "event" around the corner. But Kate did not want a father.

She'd had one, the best one, and he was gone.

Garrett couldn't replace him; nobody could.

"He's not going to be pleased when he learns, Kate," Julian warned her.

Kate nodded in silence, watching Garrett's mother walk up to him. The elderly woman said something he didn't seem to find particularly pleasant to hear, and a frown settled on his handsome face as he listened.

If only she didn't love that stubborn moron so very, very much...

"Lately he's not pleased about anything," Kate absently said. She remembered the times she'd caught him looking at her with a black scowl during the family events, and just couldn't see why he seemed so bothered with her. "And I don't want him to stop me."

Her father's job had been to protect the Gages. And he had. But somehow, with his death, the family had ended up feeling like they should protect Kate.

They'd made her feel welcome and appreciated for almost two decades. But after receiving so much for so long and giving back so little, Kate felt indebted to the family in a way that made her desperate to prove to them, to all of them, that she was an independent woman now. Especially to Garrett.

"Fair enough. Sunny Florida it is," Julian agreed.

He had always been the easiest to talk to. There was a reason everyone, possibly every female at this party other than Kate, had a little crush on Julian John.

He seized her hand and kissed her knuckles, his eyes sparkling. "I guess this means we'll be buying a beach house next door."

She laughed at that, but then sobered. "Julian. You will take care of Molly for me, won't you?"

His eyes warmed at the mention of his soon-to-be wife. "Ah, Kate, I'd die for my girl. You know that."

Kate gave him a smile that told him silently but plainly how much she adored him for that. Witnessing their love for each other and how it had started out of friendship had been surprising and inspiring, and yet also heartbreaking for Kate. She loved seeing her sister so happy, but couldn't help wish…

Wish Garrett would look at her in the way Julian looked at Molly.

Stupid, blind Garrett.

Blind to the fact that the little girl who'd grown up with him had become a woman.

Blind to the fact that she would gladly be *his* woman.

And even blinder to the fact that before he could say *yay* or *nay,* Kate Devaney was moving to Florida.

"What do you mean, Katie's moving to Florida?"

Stunned, Garrett stared in disbelief at his mother,

his date and business associate completely forgotten at his side.

"Only what I meant. Little Katie's moving to Florida. And no, there's nothing we can do about it. I already tried. And hi there," she said to the blonde pouting at his side. "What did you say your name was?"

"Cassandra Clarks." The woman extended a hand that sparkled with almost as many jewels as his mother's.

But Garrett was too preoccupied to pay attention to their sudden conversation, a conversation that was no doubt about the promising possibility of merging Clarks Communications into the Gage conglomerate. He spotted Kate across the room, and a horrible sensation wrenched through him. *She was leaving?*

When her gaze collided with his, the grip in his stomach tightened a notch. God, she looked cute as a ladybug tonight, too cute to be waltzing around in that dress without making a man sweat.

Then there were her eyes. Every time she looked up at him with those sky-blue eyes, pain sliced through his chest as though that bullet had actually hit Garrett, instead of her father. He'd never forget that he was living now, breathing now, because Kate's father had stepped into the line of fire to save him.

He'd tried to make it up to her. The entire family had. A good education, a roof over her head, help with securing her own place and encouragement so she'd open her catering business. But lately Kate seemed sad and discontent, and Garrett just didn't know how to resolve that.

He felt sad and discontent, too.

"But...she can't go," he said.

Eleanor Gage halted her conversation with Cassandra and turned her unapologetic expression up to his. "She says she can."

"To do what? Her whole *life* is here."

His mother raised a perfectly plucked brow that dared him to wonder *why,* exactly, she would want to leave, and a sudden thought occurred to him. He frowned as he considered it. Kate's distance would be good for him. He might even finally be able to get some sleep. But no. Hell, no.

He'd made a promise to her father, years ago, the tragic night of his death. Kate and her little sister, Molly, had become orphans because of Garrett. They would always belong here, with the Gages. This was their home, and Garrett had done everything in his power so that they would feel comfortable, protected and cared for.

Molly was marrying his younger brother now. But Kate?

Garrett had always had a weakness for her. He respected her. Protected her. Even from things he himself sometimes felt.

His whole life he'd ignored the way Kate's hair fell over her eyes. The way she said *Garrett* an octave lower than any other word she spoke. He'd ignored the way his chest cramped when she spoke of having a date, and he'd even done his best to try not to count all the freckles on the bridge of her pretty nose.

It wasn't easy to force himself to be so damned ignorant. Of that. But he'd done it by force and that was exactly how it would remain.

Kate was like his sister and best friend. Except she was truly neither….

No matter.

He would still do all kinds of things to protect her—

and this included making her see that moving to Florida was not a good option. Not an option, period.

Scowling, he snagged his mother by the elbow and pulled her closer, so that Cassandra didn't overhear. But the woman took the cue and easily began to mingle—leaving him to talk to his mother in peace. "When did she say she was leaving?"

"The day after the wedding."

"Eight weeks?" His brain almost ached as he tried to think of ways to keep her here. "Long enough to change her mind then."

"My darling, if you manage to—" his mother gently patted him on the chest "—you'll make me a very happy woman. I don't want Katie anywhere in the world but *here*."

Garrett bleakly agreed and snatched a wine goblet from a passing server. He almost downed the liquid in one gulp, wondering how in the hell one could change the mind of a stubborn little handful like Kate. She could teach old, grumpy men a thing or two about sticking to their guns, and Garrett wasn't looking forward to being on the opposite end of the field from her. Or then again, maybe he was.

It was always fun to pick a fight with Kate.

It seemed the only way he could vent his frustrations sometimes.

Frustrations that seemed to grow by the minute as he stalked over to Cassandra, who was engaged in a conversation with two other women Garrett knew but couldn't remember the names of.

He was interested in securing her family's company to consolidate the Gages' grip on Texas media, but he couldn't even think about that now.

Kate was packing her bags and flying out of his life in eight weeks, and he was so determined to stop that from happening that, if he had to, he would run to Florida after her on his own two feet, and come back carrying her like a sack of potatoes on his back.

Which might even be more fun than fighting with her now.

"Something's come up," he apologized as he brought the blonde around to look at him. "I'm afraid I'll need a rain check on our talk."

He smiled down at her to ease the blow, marveling that he could, and he was glad to find there was no hostility in her eyes. She didn't tell him to go take his apology and shove it where it hurt, but instead she said, sounding alarmed, "When can I see you again?"

"Soon," he said with a nod, his mind already on Kate.

Two

He spotted her out on the terrace, and his insides twisted painfully tight. Tall and slender, Kate leaned against the balcony railing outside of the French doors, peacefully gazing out at the gardens. Her dress dipped seductively in the back, exposing inches and inches of flawless bare flesh and the small, delicate little rises of her spine. Something feral and dangerous pummeled through him. *She's leaving me....*

She'd been avoiding him tonight. And now he knew why.

He clenched his hands, hauled in a breath, then yanked the doors open and stepped outside.

A warm breeze flitted by as he approached her. A slice of moon hung in the sky above her, bathing her with its silvery light. It was the kind of night lovers waited for. A night for whispers, for promising forever…

"Why?"

She spun around in a whirl of silk and red hair, her lips slightly parted, her eyes wide and bright. "Don't tell me," she said with a disappointed shake of her head. "Your mother told you."

"Why, Kate? Why am I always the last to know?"

For a moment, she didn't seem to have an answer. *She's leaving you. She's leaving you and won't tell you. Won't look at you.*

Restlessly, she pulled at her small earring as she gazed out at the majestically lit lawns. "I…uh, planned to tell you."

"From where? *Florida?*" he scoffed, unsure whether he was wounded, angry, amused or just plain damn confused.

"Okay, maybe yes, from Florida," she admitted. "But you've been grumpy lately, Garrett. I can't handle you right now. I'm too busy."

His lips twisted into a cynical smile as he leaned on the balustrade next to her. He eyed the length of her glossy hair, wondering what it would smell like up close. Raspberries in the summer…? Peaches and cream? And why in the hell did he need to know? And what did she mean, he was grumpy? "I don't *need* to be *handled*."

With a pointed stare that told him that he really *did,* Kate studied him with mischievous blue eyes. "You haven't exactly been easy to be around lately."

"Come on, I can't be that bad!"

She shot him a wry smile, and Garrett found himself responding to that captivating grin. He nudged her elbow up on thc railing. "Katc. What did you think I'd do? Tie you to your kitchen to keep you here? Steal your damn plane ticket?"

"The fact that you've already thought of that makes me wonder about your sanity."

"The fact that you're leaving makes me want to check your head, too. You belong here."

He sensed—rather than saw—the smile on her lips, but when she refused to look at him, Garrett wondered why Kate seemed so absorbed by the dark gardens it was as if she'd never seen them before—as if she'd never played outside in that yard when she was growing up. His heart jerked as an awful suspicion struck him.

"This is because of a man, isn't it?"

"Excuse me?"

"You don't just dump a life like yours and go away for nothing. So why are you running? Is it a man?"

"Does it matter?" she asked, thrusting her chin up a notch. "I'm leaving, Garrett, and I'm certain."

The rebellious note that crept into her voice only confirmed to him that it was a man.

A toad Garrett wanted to kill with his own two hands.

Pushing away from the railing with sudden force, he plunged his hands into his pants pockets and paced in a circle on the terrace, lowering his voice when he stopped at her side again. "Who's going to protect you?"

She scrunched her pretty nose with a little scoff. "I don't need protecting anymore. I'm grown up, in case you missed it."

He was struck by a memory of holding his jacket over Kate's head while they rushed into the house, soaked and laughing. They'd both been just teens. His chest turned to lead as he wondered if he'd never do that again. Laugh with her again. Laugh, period.

"Adult or baby, you still need to know that someone's got your back," he grumbled.

She glanced down at the limestone terrace floor, and for a nanosecond, he detected a flash of pain in her expression. "I know you've got my back," she said softly.

She sounded as sad as he felt, and suddenly he wanted to punch his fist into something.

Because *nothing* in his life felt right anymore.

Everything he did felt pointless. He felt restless. Angry. So angry at himself.

He imagined her all alone in a new place, with no one to help her with anything. Not if she got lost. Not if she was lonely. Not to unload her stuff. Not if there was thunder outside—she hated thunder. He clamped his jaw, loath to think of how many Florida men would be out there just ready to use and discard her, and then continued his attempt at persuasion. "What about Molly? You two are close."

"And we still will be. But Molly has Julian now. Plus she's promised to visit, and so will I."

"Then what about your catering business?"

"What about it?"

"It's taken off during the past couple of years. You worked your butt off to make it happen, Kate."

She lifted her shoulders in a casual shrug, as if leaving her entire life behind were just an everyday occurrence to her, as if she couldn't wait to leave the shadow of the Gages behind. "Beth's my associate now. Trust me, if Landon married her, it means she's very capable of handling things by herself. We'll hire a couple more helpers, and I can start a new branch in Miami."

Frustrated at her responses, he ground his molars as he thought of a thousand arguments, but he predicted she'd have a retort for each one. How in the hell was he going to change her mind?

Her smile lacked its usual playfulness as her pretty blue eyes held his. "So that's it? Those are your arguments for me staying?"

Her lips…they looked redder tonight, plumper. He wanted to touch them with his thumb and take off her lipstick. See her all fresh and pure like he was used to seeing her. Not all made up. Just pink, fresh-skinned, with those seven freckles on her nose, and that soft coral mouth that he—

Damn.

He stiffened against the heat building in his loins.

But Kate… She made him feel so damned protective it wasn't even funny. Her smiles, her personality, her alertness… There was no part of Kate he would ever change. No part of her he wouldn't miss when she left for Florida.

Luckily, she wouldn't be going anywhere.

"What am I going to do to change your mind?" he asked, more to himself than to her.

"Nothing. Honestly. My mind's completely made up."

He noticed the tray of wineglasses she'd set down nearby. She was taking a short break from making the rounds, he supposed. So he seized one and offered her another.

"Here's to me changing your mind," he said with an arrogant smile. He would find out what she was running away from, and he would eliminate it from the face of the planet.

She laughed, and the sound did magical things to him even as she declined the wine he offered her. "Oh, no, I don't drink when I'm working."

He snorted. "I should've stopped seven glasses ago, and yet here I am. Still going strong. Drink with me, Freckles."

"Well it *is* your birthday. You might as well enjoy."

"Come on. Join me on this toast. I relieve you of your duties." He pressed the glass against the back of her fingers, glad when she finally took it. He felt cocky and arrogant as he lifted his glass. "Here's to me changing your mind," he repeated.

Kate's eyes gained a new sparkle as she did the same. "And to me, and my new life in *Florida*."

They knocked glasses in toast, and it was on.

It was *on*.

Like when they were kids playing Battleship…hell, yeah. Garrett was going to sink Kate's Florida ship to the bottom of the ocean.

As though mentally plotting, too, Kate quietly sipped, watching him over the rim with a little glimmer in her eyes. A glimmer that told him she was definitely onto his plan.

Think what you want, Freckles. But you won't be going anywhere.

"I'm not backing out until I get my way, Kate. You know this, correct?" Garrett warned with a smile

Kate shook her head, but was smiling, too. "See? And you asked me why I didn't tell you? There's your answer. I can't *deal* with you right now, Garrett. I need to pack and make plans, help Molly with preparations so I can leave after the wedding."

"You don't need to *deal* with me. I will be the one dealing with *you,*" he countered as he finished his glass. He snatched another and then gazed out at the gardens, the alcohol already slowing his usually sharp brain. Oh, yes, he was determined.

He just couldn't imagine his life without Kate in it.

Every family celebration—hell, every family dinner, gathering or festivity—she would be there. Every morning in his office, her delectable croissants would be there. In his mind, his very dark soul, every second of the day, she was *there*....

"Will you be spending the night here?"

The lights in her eyes vanished at his question, and she nodded sadly. "Your mother said I could use my old room. She doesn't want me driving alone so late. You know what happened..."

To our fathers, he thought. They'd taken Garrett to watch a rock concert.

Neither had returned.

The reminder made his stomach twist and turn until he thought he'd puke.

He wanted to discuss Florida, take back control, make her promise she would stay and settle this here and now. But he didn't feel like he was in control of all five senses anymore; he'd drained the second glass already, which brought tonight's drink count to almost a dozen, so perhaps he could save this for another day.

Setting down the empty glass on the tray, he said, "All right, Kate. Sleep tight. I'll see you in the morning."

"Garrett." Her voice stopped him, and he turned from the terrace door. There was regret in her eyes, and he worried she'd see the truth of his torment in his. Then she sadly shook her head. "Happy birthday."

"You know what I want from you for my birthday, don't you?" he asked, his voice so low she'd probably barely heard it.

For a long, charged moment, their gazes held. The wind rustled the bottom of her dress and pulled tendrils of hair out of her bun. Watching the way the breeze caressed her, he felt unraveled on the inside with crazy thoughts about tucking that hair behind her ear, feeling the material of her silky dress under his fingers.

"What?" she asked, sounding breathless. "What is it that you want for your birthday?"

Her eyes had glazed over. Now her chest heaved as though his answer made her nervous and, at the same time, excited, and for a moment, Garrett felt equally nervous, and equally excited. For that fraction of a second, he just wanted to say one word, just one word, that would change their lives unequivocally in some way. But he forced himself to say the rest.

"You," he whispered, barely able to continue when he noticed the way her cheeks flushed, the way she licked her lips. "Here. I want you here on my next birthday. I want you here every day of the year. That's all I want, Kate."

You...

Kate felt strangely melancholy, lying in her old bed, in her old room, with its decorations still left over from her childhood. She didn't want to think that this was the last time she'd be sleeping here, a door away from Garrett. She didn't want to think it'd be the last birthday she spent with him and that some other guy she'd meet in Florida, a cabana boy or whatever, would be the one she'd settle down with.

She'd been barely seven when she buried her dad, and in that strange reflective moment when a grieving child gains the maturity of an old person, Kate had realized that her chance to be loved, to belong to something and someone, was now buried six feet under, in a smooth wood coffin.

She'd never blamed Garrett for anything, at least not at first.

She hadn't been told what had happened in the beginning. She'd only learned that two men had been murdered and the killers had been caught and would spend their lives behind bars. Which had seemed like such an easy punishment, compared to how her father and Garrett's had lost their lives. Garrett and his brothers had grieved their father, and Kate and Molly had quietly grieved their own. But then she had overheard a conversation Garrett's mother had had with the police, and Kate had found out what really happened. She had felt betrayed, kept from the truth by their whispers. Garrett's betrayal had hurt most of all.

She'd always had a soft spot for that dark-haired boy, and she'd felt like he hadn't even cared enough for her to tell her the truth. That her father had not died to save his dad. He had died to save Garrett. She'd rushed up to him one day and told him he should be ashamed of himself. She'd asked him how he could stand there with that poker face, and laugh, and try to pretend nothing had happened, when it had been his fault! Her father had died protecting Garrett from the gunshots. All because Garrett hadn't run for cover when he should have. She'd been angry because they'd all lied to her, to her and poor innocent Molly, who was merely three and lonely. But she had been especially angry at Garrett.

She'd regretted the words instantly, though, when she'd seen the way his neck had gone red, and his fisted hands had trembled at his sides, and his eyes had gone dead like she'd just delivered the last blow that he'd needed to join the two men down under.

The death wish the boy had developed afterward

had alarmed the family to such an extent that the Gage matron had asked Kate to please talk to him. Horribly remorseful, Kate had approached him one day and apologized. She'd realized that her father would have done that for anyone, which was true. No matter how painful it had been to speak, she'd said that it had been his job, and he had done it well. He was a hero. Her hero, and now he was gone.

Garrett had listened gravely, said nothing for long moments, and Kate had felt a new, piercing sense of loss when she realized in fear that she and Garrett would never be friends again. They would never be able to cope with this huge loss and guilt again.

"I wish it had been me."

"No! No!" She'd suddenly hated herself for having planted this in his head, for not coping well with this strange anger and neediness inside her. Maybe she'd been so angry because all she'd wanted was for someone to put his arms around her and Molly and say it would be okay, even if it was a lie and it would never be okay.

But Garrett had tossed a small twig aside, and gazed down at her hand like he'd wanted to take it. She hadn't known if she wanted him to hold it or not, but when he had, a current had rushed up her arm as if the tips of her fingers where he touched her had been struck by lightning.

"I'm gonna be your hero now," he'd said.

And he was.

He'd protected her his entire life, from anything and everything. He'd become not only her hero…but the only man she'd ever wanted.

He could feel Kate in the house somehow.

Of course his mother wouldn't let her drive so late

back to her apartment alone. Garrett also had an apartment of his own in a newer neighborhood, but tonight he'd also planned to stay in his old room so he could get blissfully inebriated without having to drive. And yet even after all the wine he'd drunk, he didn't feel so high.

The news of Kate's plans to move had sobered him.

Now he lay in bed with just a little buzz to scramble his brain, not enough to numb his thoughts. He couldn't stop thinking about her.

He might as well have been eighteen again, staring at the ceiling, sleepless with the knowledge that Kate slept nearby. Except now, Molly no longer slept in Kate's same room, and Kate wasn't a teenager anymore. Neither was Garrett.

With the vivid imagination of a man, he imagined her red hair fanning out against the white pillow, and the mere thought of her in bed caused his muscles to tighten.

His chest became heavy as he grappled with the same feelings of guilt and solitude that he always did when he thought of her.

Garrett had also denied little Molly of a father. But Molly had never looked at him with resentment. She had never really looked at him like she *wanted* something from him, like Kate did.

Sometimes, when he got drunk and reflective, he wondered if that night had never happened, would things have been different for him? He might have been happier, like his younger brother. He could have also waited until Kate was the right age, and then, if there had been any hint of her having any special feelings for him, he might have let himself feel them back for her. But it was pointless to imagine it. Pointless torture and torment.

Because that night *had happened,* and Garrett could still feel the dank air, hear the gunshots and remember it as if it had happened less than twenty-four hours ago.

Yeah, he remembered exactly how those gunshots had exploded so close to him, how they'd burst between the buildings of downtown San Antonio like an echo. He remembered his father's grip—which had been firm on Garrett as he guided him into the concert entrance—and how suddenly he'd jerked at his side and his fingers had let go. His father had crashed like a deadweight to the asphalt.

"Dad?" Garrett had said, paralyzed in confusion for a second, only to be instantly shoved aside by Dave Devaney, whose expression clearly told Garrett he'd already figured out what was going on.

"Get down—run!" the man had shouted, reaching for the weapon Garrett knew he carried inside his jacket. But Garrett could hear his father sputtering, struggling to breathe, and he had been paralyzed for a stunned moment. The world could have been crashing over him. As far as he'd known, it had been. But all he had been conscious of was his father. In the middle of the street, clutching his chest, where blood spurted through his open fingers like a fountain.

Instead of running away, Garrett had run back to him. He hadn't known what he planned to do. He'd only known his father was covered in blood, choking on his own breath, and that his eyes—dark as coal like Garrett's—looked wild and frightened. As wild and frightened as Garrett felt.

He'd dived back for the figure on the ground and gripped him by one arm, trying to drag him aside, when he'd heard Devaney's "No, boy! Dammit, no!" A half dozen more gunshots had exploded, and in that instant, the weight of a man had crushed him to the ground.

Garrett had cursed in front of his father for the first time in his life and squirmed between both men. Something hot and sticky had oozed across both his chest and back as he'd tried to push free, which had proved immensely difficult being he was only ten, and Dave Devaney had been a big man. His father had sputtered one last time beneath him, and when Garrett swung his head around, Jonathan Gage's eyes had been lifeless.

Garrett had gone cold, listening to sirens in the distance, footsteps, chaos around them.

Suddenly he'd heard Dave's voice, saying, "Garrett," as he rolled to the side to spare Garrett his weight. He'd blinked up at the man, shocked, mute when he realized the man had stepped into the line of fire to save him. Him. Who hadn't run when he'd been told to.

The man had reached out to pat his jaw, and Garrett had grabbed the man's hand and attempted a reassuring squeeze. He'd shaken uncontrollably, felt sticky and startlingly cold. "My daughters… They have no one but me. No one but me. Do you understand me, boy?"

He'd nodded wildly.

The man had seemed to struggle to swallow. To speak and breathe. But his eyes had had that wild desperation Garrett's father had worn, except his gaze had also been pleading. Pleading with Garrett. "Help me…. Be there…for them…"

He'd nodded wildly again.

"So that they are not alone…taken care of…safe. Tell 'em…I l-love…"

Garrett had nodded, his face wet and his eyes scalding hot as he tried to reassure the dying man. His chest had hurt so much he'd thought he'd been shot, as well. "Yes, sir," he'd said low, with the conviction of a ten-year-old who'd suddenly aged to eighty. "I'll take care of them both."

But how *could* he take care of Kate now, if they would be miles and states apart?

Kate was jolted from her thoughts when the door of her bedroom crashed open. She sat upright on the bed, her heart hammering in her chest. A huge shadow loomed at the threshold.

Garrett.

"I don't want you to leave," he said gruffly.

Shock widened her eyes. His voice was slurred, and she wondered how many more drinks he'd had after they'd last seen each other.

From the light of the hall, she could see he was still partly dressed in his black slacks and button-up shirt. His tie was loose around his collar. His hair rumpled. His sleeves rolled up. Oh, God, he looked adorable.

"I've made up my mind," she told him.

"Then unmake it."

He shut the door behind him and strode into the darkness, and her heart beat faster in response.

"I can't unmake it," she said, her voice raspy. Her throat was aching and she thought that the night of no sleep yesterday and the marathon to get everything set up today had just set her up to fall ill. "Look, I made up my mind. I can't stay here."

"Why?"

"Because I'm unhappy, Garrett. I've got everything I ever wanted, and yet don't. I make money for myself,

I've got great friends, and Molly, and I've got you and your family…and I'm so unhappy."

The mattress squeaked as he sat down, and suddenly she felt his hand patting the bed as though to find her. "Why are you unhappy?" he asked. He found her thigh over the covers, and when he squeezed, her stomach tightened, too.

She couldn't remember ever being in a dark room with him, or maybe she could, decades ago, when he had been sick and she would help Eleanor nurse him and feed him soup. But now she was no longer a girl. Her body was a woman's, and her responses to this man were purely feminine and decidedly discomforting. Her blood raced hot through her veins as her body turned the same consistency of her pillow behind her. Soft. Feathery. Weightless.

"Why are you unhappy?" he murmured. She felt the mattress squeak again when he edged closer. He seemed to be palpating the air until he felt her shoulder; then he slid his hand up her face. The touch of his fingers melted her, and she closed her eyes as he cupped her jaw and bent to her ear. "Tell me what makes you unhappy and I'll fix it for you."

He smelled of alcohol. And his unique scent.

She shook her head at his impossible proposition, almost amused, but not quite. More like unsettled. By his nearness, his touch.

She had promised herself, when she'd decided she had to move away, that she would forget this man. And now all she could think of was reaching up to touch his hair and draw his lips to hers. She couldn't see him in the darkness, but she knew his face by memory. The sleek line of his dark eyebrows. The beautiful tips of his sooty eyelashes. The strikingly beautiful espresso shade of his eyes, dark brown from up close and coal-black from afar.

She knew his strong face, with that strong, proud forehead, as strong as his cheekbones and jaw, and she knew the perfect shape of his mouth. She might not have touched his face with her fingers in her life, but her eyes had run over those features more than they had touched any other thing on this earth.

"You can't fix it. You're not God," she sadly whispered. Her throat now ached with emotion, too.

"You're right. I'm a devil." He cupped her face in both hands and stroked his thumb across the flesh of her lips, triggering a strange reaction in her body. "Why did you wear lipstick tonight? You look prettier bare."

Her breath caught as she realized he was stroking her lips with his thumb like he wanted to kiss her. He'd called her pretty. When had he ever called her pretty? Decades ago, maybe by accident, he'd blurted it out. But it had been years since he'd ever complimented her. Or touched her.

He'd just done both.

And suddenly the only thing moving in the room was her heaving chest, and his thumb as it moved side to side, caressing her lips, filling her body with an ocean of longing. She swallowed back a moan.

"You're right to want to leave here, Kate." His voice thickened as he bent his head, and he smelled so good and exuded such body warmth and strength, she went light-headed. "You should run from here."

It took every ounce of willpower for her to push at his hard shoulders. "You're drunk, Garrett. Go away and get out of my bed."

His hands tightened on her face as he nuzzled her

nose with his, the timbre of his voice rough with torment. "Kate, there's not a day I don't remember what I took from you—"

"Garrett, we can talk about all this tomorrow."

"There's nothing to discuss. You're staying here. *Here,* Kate. Where I can take care of you and I know you're safe. All right, Freckles?"

"Even if I'm miserable?"

He dropped his hands to her shoulders and squeezed. "Tell me what makes you miserable, Kate. I'll take care of it. I'll make it better for you."

Kate wanted to push him away, *needed* to push him away. He was drunk and she didn't have the energy to deal with him tonight, not like this. But the instant she flattened her palms on his shirt, they stayed there. On his chest. Feeling his hard muscles through the fabric, his heart beating under her hands. Between her legs, she grew moist and hot.

When she was little, she'd wanted him because he was strong and protective, and her favorite boy of all the boys she'd ever met. But now she was older and a new kind of wanting tangled up inside her. Her breasts went heavy from the mere act of touching his chest through his shirt, and her nipples puckered against her nightshirt.

"Do me a favor, Kate?"

His voice slurring even more, Garrett sounded drunker by the second as he stroked her face with unsteady fingertips. Every pore in her body became aware of that whispery touch, causing shivers down her nerve endings.

"Stay with us. My mother loves you. Beth loves you, and so does her son." He seemed to wrack his brain for more to say. "And Molly. Molly loves you, Kate. She needs you. Julian, Landon, hell, everyone."

But not him?

She didn't know if she wanted to laugh or cry or hit him for excluding himself, but she already knew that she was a weight on him, a responsibility to him. That's what she'd always been. Forcing her arms to return to her sides, she sighed. "Garrett…"

"What will that obsessed client of yours, Missy Something, do without your currant muffins? What will I do? Hmm, Kate? It's a tragedy to think about it."

"I don't want to argue about this now, Garrett." She rubbed her temple.

"All right, Katie."

She blinked.

"All right?" she repeated.

Confused by his easy concession, which was not like Garrett at all, she suddenly heard him shift on the bed and spread his big body down the length beside her.

Eyes widening in horror, she heard him plump one of the two pillows.

"All right, Katie. We'll talk about it in the morning," he said in that deep, slurred voice.

She heard him shift once more, as if to get more comfortable. Sitting on the bed, frozen in disbelief, she managed to sputter, "You're not planning to *stay* here the night, are you?"

He made a move with his head that she couldn't see but rustled the pillow.

"Garrett, you moron, go to your *room,*" she said, shoving at his arm a little.

He caught her hand and squeezed it. "Relax, you little witch. I'll go back to my room when I stop spinning. Come here and brace me down." He draped his arm around her shoulders and drew her to his side, and Kate was too stunned to do anything but play rag doll.

Minutes passed as she remained utterly still, every part of her body excruciatingly aware of his powerful arm. Garrett was not the touchy-feely brother; that was Julian. In fact, Garrett seemed to do his best not to touch her. But his guard was down and he seemed not to want to let *go* this time.

She frowned when he tightened his hold and slid his fingers up beneath the fall of her hair. Cupping her scalp, he pressed her face down to his chest.

"Garrett," Kate said, poking on his abs. They were hard as rocks under his shirt.

He breathed heavily. Oh, no. Seriously. Was he asleep?

"Garrett?"

She groaned when there was no response and wondered if she should move into Garrett's room and leave him to sleep here, because she was certainly not dragging him to his own room. He must weigh double what she did, even if he was all muscle, judging from the hardness of the arm around her and the abs she'd just poked.

Instead, she grumbled and complained under her breath, and ended up using her pillow as a barrier between them. She eased his arm from around her, setting it on the pillow. His hand was enormous between her fingers, and for a moment, she seemed to be unable to let go, kept her hand over his just to feel that he was not a figment of her imagination. Then she realized what she was doing and that it was stupid and foolish, and she yanked her hand away.

Damn him.

He was going to do everything possible to keep her in Texas, she knew.

But he wasn't going to take Florida away from her.

Oh, no, her life had stopped revolving around Garrett Gage ever since she'd decided she didn't want him anymore, and now she'd be damned before she let him screw up her perfect plans, too.

Three

Monday morning, business at the *San Antonio Daily* was more intense than normal.

Usually Landon, the eldest Gage brother, would bark about the grammar mistakes in that day's print edition. Julian John, the youngest, was no longer working at headquarters since he'd started his own PR firm, but he still occasionally dropped in and offered his services in weekly status meetings. Lately, Garrett had been focused on maneuvering their assets to make one of their greatest takeovers, one that would absorb Clarks Communications into the *Daily* and the rest of their holdings.

Which was why Cassandra Clarks was visiting today. She sat in Garrett's office, quietly eating the remaining muffin from the batch Kate had sent to the office this morning.

It made Garrett grumpy to see that muffin go.

But he feigned indifference as he flipped to the next page of the current stock statistics for Clarks Communications. Still, he wasn't really paying attention to their impressive growth numbers. Instead, he kept going back to Saturday night and Sunday morning.

He'd woken up alone, dressed in the most uncomfortable way possible, with a stiff back and the scent of Kate in bed, which had made him hard as marble.

Then he'd realized he was lying on Kate's old, frilly pink bed. Which he'd apparently decided to take over during the night while on a semidrunken spree.

Damn.

He'd immediately texted her Sunday morning, and even now, he kept glancing at his phone, replaying their conversation.

Sorry for crashing in last night.

You mean that was you? That's all right, at least u didn't break anything.

But my pride. And my back.

Ouch. Ok, but it's nothing my muffins won't cure.

Holy hell. Was she flirting with him?

I'm going to savor every bite.

He wasn't sure if he'd been flirting, too. *Savor every bite.* The alcohol had still been running through his system, clearly messing up his head. Thank God Kate hadn't replied after that last one. But she'd sent a dozen muffins this morning and he had gobbled three up with barely a drink of coffee. His experience with Kate's food was almost sexual.

He couldn't help it; it had always been like this since the beginning.

The first time she'd made chocolate-chip cookies on her own, Garrett had been fresh out of bed on a Sunday in his randy teen years. He'd been scouring the kitchen for breakfast and had shoved a warm cookie into his mouth, nodding when she'd asked if it was good. Then Kate had laughingly stepped up and brushed a crumb from the side of his mouth, and he'd almost swallowed the cookie whole.

Sometimes he waited until he was alone to eat her stuff. And he imagined he was licking her fingers when he wrapped his tongue around her sugary frostings. And when they had little sprinkles, he pictured her freckles.

He really should look into therapy.

Suddenly he heard Landon sigh and slap his copy of the report shut, and he was jerked back to the present.

"So if your brother is still not aware of our plans," he asked Cassandra, "why are you chickening out on selling?" The chair creaked as he leaned back, folding his arms over his chest.

Cassandra Clarks may have had the appearance of a blonde bombshell, but behind that "bimbo" facade, Garrett had learned, there was actually a brain. The woman was not only smart, but about as flexible on her terms as a damned wall.

Today she exuded casual confidence, slowly shaking her head as Landon explained his position.

"We're supposed to keep buying the stock until we get over twenty percent," Landon told her. "In a week, two at most, your brother's company will be ours before he even realizes we're in bed with him. No pun intended."

"None taken," Cassandra said, eyeing Landon judiciously as she finally stopped shaking her head and allowed him to continue.

"Once we secure your remaining thirty-two percent, it puts us in control, and it leaves you a very wealthy woman, Cassie."

"That's the problem. My brother will know I sold to you. He will destroy me and anything else I have," she said, her entire countenance clouded with worry. "What I wanted to propose to Garrett on Saturday before he cut me short was a marriage of convenience. My brother has control of my stake in the company now, but if I marry, he won't have control over financial decisions regarding my stake anymore. My husband can take over the shares and compensate me discreetly. It would be an easy arrangement, and over in six months, where we'll both happily walk away with what we want. Me with my money, you with the stock."

Garrett remained silent as he absorbed the proposal. He met Cassandra's gaze unflinchingly, the ambitious businessman in him wanting to say yes. But in his mind, he went back to waking up to Kate's scent on the pillow, to the memory of somehow holding her in his arms.

He tugged at the collar of his shirt several times, aware that his frown was pinching into his face. "I'm afraid that's not an option, Cassandra," he said, signaling for his assistant to refill all their coffees.

Hell, he might even start drinking whiskey at this hour. Because *marriage?*

"Like Landon said, we're willing to buy those shares up front. No need to get dramatic about it."

“I’m afraid selling out front is not an option. My brother is… You don’t know him. Marriage is the only way I can free myself of his control. You take the shares, transfer the money to me, and then we walk six months later with irreconcilable differences. It’s a marriage in name only and we have nothing to lose. That’s the only way it’s happening: you marry me and by right take my thirty-two percent.”

Landon’s and Garrett’s eyes met across the conference table. Landon’s gray gaze almost looked silver in his concern.

“Look, Cassandra,” he started. “We’re almost at twenty percent already. We’ll buy your position outright at way above market price. At fifty-two percent, we’ll be in control and can get your brother out of there. He won’t have a say in the matter anymore.”

She shook her head, her eyes tearing up. “You don’t know him. He has a say in a lot of things in my life. I don’t get real financial independence until I marry—can’t you understand?”

She reached across the table and squeezed Garrett’s hand as if she were falling from a precipice and he’d been appointed the task of hauling her up.

“It’ll be a marriage in name only, but I can make it sweet for you. I can. I know I’m pretty. I think you’re an incredibly sexy man.”

His stomach turned, and he was amazed at how calmly he looked back at her. Several years ago, he’d probably have done it without thinking. He was a businessman, after all. She was an attractive woman offering something and he had nothing to lose. People got married and divorced for other reasons; why not for business?

He just didn’t have the energy for it right now. What

he'd told Kate at his party had been the truth. All he wanted was for Kate to be home. He would dedicate every waking moment to making that happen. Life without Kate to him was…unimaginable.

He was selfish when it came to her.

He was stupid, unreasonable and stubborn when it came to her.

But Cassandra Clarks didn't know this. She didn't know that as he sat in this chair, and let her squeeze his hand, every cell in his body was burning with yearning for another woman. He'd burned for so many years, it was a miracle he hadn't turned to ashes by now.

"We'll talk about this during the week, see what we can come up with," Landon finally said. In silence, the Gage brothers both stood up to dismiss her.

Cassandra went over to shake Landon's hand, and then returned to Garrett, giving him a hug that crushed all of her assets against his chest. He could see she was trying very hard to look seductive, but he saw fear and frustration glowing in the depths of her eyes as she eased back.

Cassandra was blonde and beautiful, and she also appeared desperate. If Garrett had an ounce of mercy in him at all, he'd find a way to help her. "You'll let me know?" she asked hopefully.

He nodded. "You'll hear from us in a week or two."

"Marriage," Garrett grumbled as the door closed behind her. He fell back on his chair and rubbed his temples as he tried to think of a way they could free Cassandra from her brother's grip and get their hands on Clarks Communications.

"In name only," Landon said, gazing out the window with a thoughtful frown.

"I'm not interested in a fake marriage, Lan."

Landon sighed and spun around, coming back to the table. "Do you have any other ideas?"

Garrett lifted his shoulders. "We find another fish in the pond, let go of Clarks," he said bitterly, glaring down at his coffee.

The silence that followed made it clear that neither Landon nor he was ecstatic at the possibility. Clarks was the biggest fish in their pond, and if they were smart—which the Gage brothers were—they would secure it at all costs.

When evaluating the big picture, six months wasn't a lot of time, if it meant getting Clarks into their pocket. And Garrett had everything riding on this project. Currently, Clarks posed a threat. But once they'd acquired the company, it would be a huge asset for the Gage conglomerate.

But at the cost of a fake wedding?

Hell, it's not like you plan to ever marry. Why not at least do some business?

The two large doors of the conference room knocked open, and in strode Julian John, casual as could be, blond and Hollywoodesque, an hour after the scheduled meeting time. Behind him, one of the secretaries rushed to close the doors.

Jules never said good-morning, but then they were brothers. They didn't have to.

He regarded the pair of somber men seated at the conference table and remained standing. "I had something to do, so drop the long faces, both of you."

Landon arched a challenging brow and leaned back in his chair. "I hope it was business and not you playing around while we try to take over Clarks Communications."

"Do you even remember I no longer work here? I'm here to offer my assistance, that's all. Molls needed me this morning."

"Tell Molly to leave the baby-making for the evening," said Landon with a devilish smile.

Heading to his chair, Julian rolled his eyes at his brother. "I picked up some medicine for Kate, idiot, after Molly took her to the doctor. And if I want to make babies in the morning with my Molls, I sure as hell will make them without your permi—"

"What the hell is wrong with Kate? Is she sick?"

Julian's attention swung back to Garrett, and his blond eyebrows flew upward. "Why? Are you a doctor?"

"Is Kate," Garrett slowly enunciated, "sick? Ill? Feeling badly?"

Julian's eyes twinkled like they did when he was up to no good. "Don't you think it's about time you did something about how you feel for her, Dr. Garrett?"

"I feel responsible for her, that's how I feel," he gritted out. "And right now I'm going to punch your face if you don't tell me what's wrong with her."

Plopping into his chair, Julian grabbed his folder and started scanning the contents. "She's running a fever. A high fever. Molly took her home to stay with her, and I was the guy who picked up the prescription and dropped it off."

Garrett's overwhelming protectiveness surged with a vengeance. Kate was never sick. Ever. He didn't like knowing she was sick at all, and now, he felt sick inside. "I could've picked it up for her."

"And tear you away from Cassandra Clarks and our

plans for world domination?" Julian said. "No, bro. If that girl is selling anything, she'll sell it to you. I saw her with you at your party. I think she digs you even if you don't dig her."

"She digs him enough to marry him." Landon filled his brother in, then broached the topic currently setting Garrett's brain on overdrive. "Is Kate still planning to move to Miami?"

"As far as I know, nothing has changed her mind. But Molly's privately freaking out about it," Julian said, his expression going somber. Garrett knew his younger brother was intensely territorial and protective of Molly, and even if he was usually cool as a cucumber, it must irk him not to be able to do anything to spare her any pain.

"So is Beth," Landon murmured sadly.

Garrett looked down at the conference table and scowled. Nobody in this goddamned world could be as freaked out about it as he was.

He pictured Kate in Miami, sick and alone. Who would take her to the doctor? Who would even know that she was sick? The thought was so disturbing he pulled at his tie, feeling choked to death.

But as much as he loathed that she was sick today, maybe this would provide an opportunity to make Kate see how indispensable family that protected and cared for you was. Also, her stubbornness might be at a low point because of the fever, and he might be able to talk to her without putting her on the defensive.

"You guys don't mind if I take the rest of the day off? If there's even a chance of making her stay, I need to filter through her defenses and find out why the hell she wants to *leave*."

"You mean you want to bulldoze through her walls,

without any tact whatsoever, and screw everything?" Julian teased.

"Jules, I happen to think Kate is the one who's bulldozed through Garrett's defenses with her imminent departure," Landon said.

Both his brothers looked terribly amused.

Garrett shoved his arms into his jacket and grabbed his iPhone. "Screw you. You guys know how hotheaded Kate is when she gets something in her mind—at least today she won't have all the energy to fight me. Hell, you took two months off for your honeymoon, Landon, and you don't even work here anymore. Jules. I'm taking a day off, no matter what you both have to say."

Julian answered, with a laugh, "We have a lot to say about it, bro. We just won't be saying it to you."

"So I know you're going to find all sorts of things wrong with my stupid soup, but it's still chicken and broth and I'm not the baker here, okay, Kate?"

Molly set the tray with the steaming bowl on a chair by the window and parted the drapes.

Kate almost hissed as she raised her hand to shield herself from the sunlight.

"Wow. You look so bad, Kate."

Molly's blue eyes brimmed with sisterly pity as Kate sat up in bed and tried to peel her sweaty T-shirt off her skin. The cotton was soaked from when the fever had started dropping during her nap. Her hair was plastered to the sides of her face as if with glue.

"I feel worse than I look, I guarantee," Kate rasped out, her throat raw.

She had strep throat. Which meant she had nausea, a

throat that ached like hell and a fever that was kicking her fanny. *Wonderful.*

"Let me run a bath for you."

Molly disappeared into the bathroom, and Kate groaned when she heard the loud chime of the doorbell.

"I'll get that, Kate. Don't even move a finger. I'll be back in a bit. In the meantime, you can eat my sucky soup," Molly said, poking her head back into the bedroom. Kate smiled weakly and nodded.

As her little sister went down the hall to the front door, Kate marveled at how sharp and efficient she was being.

Molly had always been a red-hot mess, but today Kate truly felt Molly's motherly instincts surge to the forefront as she tried to pamper her big sis.

It was a rare event when Kate succumbed to being sick. She just didn't have time for it. What the hell was wrong with her?

The stress of her move had her sleepless and anxious and now, apparently, had left her with no defenses against strep.

Sighing and plopping back on her pillow, she heard voices in the living room. Then she heard footsteps approaching. Kate opened her eyes, and her stomach dropped when she saw him.

The last man she wanted to see.

Or to be more precise, the last man she wanted to see *her* like this.

She flew upright to a sitting position, her cheeks warming in an awful blush when Garrett stopped at the threshold. Her blood bubbled in her veins, and the feeling was unbidden and unwanted. He looked positively beautiful, his shoulders about a yard wide, his patterned tie slightly undone. His dark hair stood up on end as if he'd been pulling at it on his drive over.

He was honestly the most beautiful thing she'd seen all day.

She indulged in a small moment of grief as she realized that while he looked so excellent, she'd never looked worse.

"Did you lose your GPS? Your office is the other way," she said, merely because attitude was the only thing she had left now.

"I followed another compass today." A tender look warmed his eyes as he stepped inside and shut the door behind him.

He removed his jacket, and her pulse jumped at each flex of his muscles under his snowy shirt.

"How do you feel, Freckles?" He draped his jacket on the back of her desk chair and rolled his sleeves to his elbows. "We should've made you drink tequila Saturday. That would've killed anything off."

All the grogginess fled from her when he seized the tray with the soup and brought it to the bed.

"Molly suggests you eat her sucky soup."

Kate grimaced. "I'm not hungry, Garrett," she said in her slightly raspy strep-throat voice. "There's no need to check up on me."

He settled down on the edge of the bed and lifted the spoon, his eyes glimmering in pure devil-like mischief. "Starve the virus, feed the fever."

"And that means, Confucius…?"

"You need to feed your immune system. Come on. Open your mouth."

After a brief hesitation, she parted her lips and Garrett offered her the soup. Her stomach was warmed by the intent look on Garrett's face as she curled her lips around the spoon. He tipped it back, and she swallowed. Then he lowered the spoon, watching her.

"It's not that bad," she said. The soup slid down her throat and coated her sore spots. "But it's still a little too hot."

He immediately set the tray at the foot of the bed. "Molls said you're about to take a bath? Would you like to hop in there now?"

Before she could even nod, he disappeared into the bathroom, where she heard the water stop, and then he returned. He looked so sexy but at the same time, so domesticated; she almost felt giddy at all this sweet male attention.

"While you relax in your bath, I'll go get my laptop and briefcase, all right?" He signaled toward the window at his Audi parked outside. "Since she's having such success as an artist, I told Molly I'd stay here so she could go to her studio and finish up her pending works before the wedding."

"Wh-what? No! No! I don't need a babysitter!"

"Good because I didn't hire one." The smile he shot her was rather wolfish, and he looked very damned pleased about himself. "It's just you and me now. I can see you're excited about it."

"As I am about having strep!" she countered.

He burst out laughing, and once again she felt things she didn't really want to feel. Kate was going to kill her sister. Kill her. But of course Molly must've been thrilled about this turn of events. She kept insisting that Kate should stay in town until some miracle happened and Kate and Garrett finally became an item. *Ha.* She was clearly still such an innocent.

And right now, especially, not even a miracle would make someone want Kate. Only a thing called strep throat wanted her.

And just then, she remembered the exquisite feel of Garrett, big and warm, in bed with her Saturday night.

As the thought rushed through her, Kate ducked her head to hide her blush, never wanting Garrett to know the effect he had on her. On the night of his birthday, she'd been so angry and frustrated. She'd felt all kinds of unwanted arousal while he'd slept soundly next to her. So she'd promised herself she would get over him. And she would. No matter what. She merely wished that he, of all the men in the world, hadn't seen her in this state.

"You want help getting to the tub?" He gestured toward the bathroom. She was still in bed, holding the sheets to the top of her neck like a shield.

"I can walk," she answered the moment she realized how silly she must look. Frowning in annoyance at her own prudish attitude, she kicked the sheets aside, then realized that her T-shirt had ridden up to her hips. As she struggled out of bed, Garrett got a perfect view of her pink panties.

He whipped his eyes away, but not before she saw that he *saw*. Her pink panties. And her toned thighs.

Garrett's face hardened instantly, and he rubbed the nape of his neck as Kate felt a red-hot flush creep up her body.

"So, you have strep?" he asked, looking away quickly.

"It's very contagious. You should leave." In fact, she'd probably even had it incubating when he'd slept in her bed the other night. The thought of giving him strep made her insides twist in foreboding. "You should really leave, Garrett."

"I'll leave when your fever's gone, Katie."

Groaning in disgust at his stubbornness, she went into the bathroom and locked the door behind her. Oddly, she felt acutely aware of her nakedness when she stripped. Aware, also, of only one measly door separating her from him.

After double-checking the lock, she settled in the tub. The water felt so warm. She closed her eyes and sighed as she dunked her head and slowly surfaced, starting to relax.

As the minutes passed, she couldn't stop wondering what Garrett was doing out in her room. She definitely heard noises, and she figured he must be setting up a miniature office. The thought both annoyed her and… didn't. He looked extremely good today. But she couldn't help but wonder what the purpose of this sudden attention was. Of course something sneaky was going on. She had no doubt this all had to do with her leaving for Florida—and Garrett intending to convince her not to.

No way are you going to stop me, Garrett Gage.

She scowled at the thought. She hadn't even had boyfriends because of him. Directly or indirectly, he'd been responsible for Kate waiting to lose her virginity until she was over twenty-one and then she'd lost it to someone she didn't even like all that much. Even then, though, she'd kept expecting him to one day realize they were meant for each other. Now she was determined to stop waiting for anything Garrett-related.

Fiercely resolved, she came out minutes later, wrapped in a towel, bathed, refreshed and wet.

She found, not to her surprise, that Garrett was already settled in her room. He lounged back in a chair with his laptop open on her small desk before him. He'd also turned the chair so that it was facing the bed, rather than the window. He looked as out of place in her feminine bedroom as a bear would.

He glanced up when she padded barefoot toward her dresser, and an irresistibly devastating grin appeared on his face. "You already look better."

"Actually, I feel tons better." Clutching the towel to her chest, she rummaged through her drawers and was about to try to get dressed under the towel when she remembered to say, "Look away for a second, please."

As she selected her new panties, purple this time, she asked, "Are you looking away?"

"What do you think, Kate?" he asked, annoyed.

She took that as a yes and quickly let the towel drop and slipped into her panties. Even though he was looking away, her cheeks flushed red at the thought of him being so close when she was naked. She quickly slipped on her bra, still feeling hot inside, but then she realized he would probably be as moved by her nakedness as a sofa. The man was completely immune to her.

Then again, her butt was quite nice thanks to her Pilates classes. As she was thinking these thoughts and smoothing her panties over the curves in question, a strange silence settled in the room.

Garrett's voice was deceptively calm when she reached into her drawer again.

"Did you really think I'd look away, Kate?"

Kate's stomach clenched, but she went about the task of selecting a T-shirt.

And now she could feel his eyes were definitely on her.

Boring holes into her bottom, actually.

And suddenly she really prayed that it was, indeed, a very nice bottom.

"Please don't tell me you were looking," she threatened, starting to panic. She broke out into a fresh sweat as the fever continued dropping after her bath.

As she grabbed a T-shirt with a Minnie Mouse image on the front and pulled it on, she heard a deep male groan.

"Freckles, I'm not made of stone you know."

Garrett sounded grumpy, as if he was in danger of getting strep, too.

"Really? I thought you were." Instead of being embarrassed, she was suddenly amused as she pulled the T-shirt as low as possible and turned around. But her smile froze on her face.

Garrett sat like a marble statue on the chair, his muscled arms crossed, his forearms corded with veins, his lips hard and completely unsmiling. His face was harsh with intensity, and his eyes were the blackest she'd ever seen them. There was such an unearthly sheen in them, Kate stopped breathing.

They stared at each other for a heart-stopping moment, and the atmosphere seemed to morph, becoming heavy and thick with something inexplicable. There was a deeper significance to their stare that she couldn't quite pinpoint, but it felt like a delicate thread between them was pulling tight.

It hurt. This strange link. It felt threatening.

It hurt, and ached in all kinds of places inside her.

Garrett put his forehead in his hand for a moment, then sighed and ran a big, tanned hand down his face in pure frustration. "Look, Katie."

"Look, Garrett, you need to stop this now."

"Stop what?"

They stared once more, and the atmosphere in the room continued feeling heavy and odd. Kate's nerves could barely handle it.

"I know what you're trying to do, and it's not going to work," she finally said.

His eyes remained almost predatory in their intensity. Finally he raised one sleek black eyebrow. "My plot to save the world, to keep Kate in Texas, won't work, even if I put in some good hours of doctoring time?"

"It won't work."

"So you didn't mean it the night of my birthday when you said that we would talk about it later?"

"We'd both been drinking. Whatever we said that night was the alcohol talking."

"All right, so today the strep is talking. When is Kate going to talk to me?"

"I'm talking to you now."

His eyebrows fell low over his eyes. His shirt stretched over his square shoulders as he sat back, his muscled arms still crossed over his chest. "Then tell me if you're leaving because of a man. First. And second, you're going to tell me who."

"Ha. This is my house. I run it. So I say who has firsts and seconds here, not you."

She bent to put on some socks. A rivulet of water slid along her toned legs, and when she straightened, she saw his eyes had darkened even more. He continued to stare at her legs for a wildly erotic moment.

Her pulse jumped at the thought of him touching her—of him even *wanting* to touch her—and her hands trembled as she bent her head and slowly wrapped the discarded towel around her wet hair.

When she straightened, Garrett's expression had turned bleak as a funeral, and he pushed to his feet, stalking over like a pissed-off predator. "What do you need so you can get back in the damned bed, Kate?"

"I don't want to get into bed. I've been there all day. My fever is dropping and I'm sweating. I feel hot."

"Then put something on, would you!" He signaled at her long legs, and a wash of feminine awareness swept through her when his eyes raked her up and down as if he couldn't help himself.

She laughed nervously and glanced away so that he wouldn't notice his effect on her; then she hopped into a comfortable pair of white cotton shorts she used for yoga sometimes.

Garrett seemed completely disturbed and grumpy… but more than that, he seemed alert. Did this mean she'd finally gotten past one of Garrett's walls?

She almost laughed. She'd always tried many subtle ways to get his male attention. Who would have thought she just needed to do a little striptease?

It's too late, Kate. You don't want him anymore. You want a new start—without him.

Turning in sudden annoyance, she shoved at his chest so he stepped out of her personal space. "Just go home, Garrett. You don't have to do this. Aren't you working on that big deal all your brothers are talking about?"

He looked agitated and started pacing around, scowling down at the carpet. "There's nothing I can do about it today. We're ironing out the details."

"Well, go iron them out somewhere else."

"On the bed, Freckles! Unless you like your soup cold!"

With a complaining sound, Kate plopped down on the

bed and crossed her legs under her body. He expelled a breath, as if finally appeased; he was just so handsome her heart ached. She propped her head back on the headboard as he brought back the tray, and she quietly studied him as he fed her.

Garrett Gage was one of the least emotionally accessible men Kate had ever met, and to see him do something so honestly sweet for her triggered a wealth of unreasonable emotions in her chest.

She didn't want to feel giddy and protected and cared for. But she did. She felt safe. And fiercely achy for so much more. His dark espresso eyes wouldn't stop watching her mouth as he guided the spoon inside, and out, and it made every time she wrapped her lips around the spoon unbearably…intimate.

Suddenly all she could hear was the sound of their breathing in the bedroom. Hers was not all that steady. His was inexplicably slow and deep, his chest extending slowly under his shirt as those dark, thick-lashed, half-mast eyes remained on her face.

"Poor Jules. I swear Molly doesn't cook for anything," Kate whispered, anxious to break the silence.

Now that she was able to taste the soup better, she definitely knew her little sister could use a little cooking advice from her.

Garrett chuckled. The sound was rich and male as he set down the spoon. "He's in love with her, Katie. She can feed him cotton balls and he'll be content."

"I love how they love each other."

Suddenly feeling drained, she shook her head when Garrett offered more soup. She slid down the bed a little so that the back of her head could rest on her pillow.

The thought of Julian and Molly made the ache in her chest multiply tenfold.

"They're not afraid to," she added.

Garrett didn't respond. He merely set the tray aside and turned thoughtfully back to her. "I wouldn't let fear keep me from someone," he said then, his voice a low murmur.

"No? Then what would?"

His powerful shoulders lifted in a noncommittal shrug, and then he said, "If you love someone, you want what's best for them. Even if it means it's not you."

Something in his words caused a little ribbon of pain to unravel within her. Had he ever felt anything for her, and thought that he wasn't good enough for her?

No. How could he not be good enough for anyone? He was honorable and dedicated, fiercely passionate about those he loved, as protective as an angry panther.

"Garrett, you don't have to stay. I know you told Molly you would but I'd rather you go," she said, getting sleepier by the second. "The antibiotics and steroids make me dizzy anyway, so I'll probably sleep all afternoon. And if you stay here I'm going to give you strep."

The tenderness that liquefied his gaze suddenly made her feel even more soft and languid. "You're not giving me anything. Relax and I'll be here when you wake up."

His voice was so soothing and gentle she couldn't help but nod and close her eyes. As she heard him take the tray to the kitchen, she snuggled into her pillow, her stomach warmed with Molly's sucky soup, which, even if tasteless, had served its purpose well. Ever since Molly had moved in with Julian, the house had seemed so quiet. Just knowing Garrett was around right now made her feel safe and protected.

The steroids were kicking in as well as the antibiotics, and her fever seemed to be breaking.

New beads of perspiration popped onto her brow, and a new, unexpected heaviness settled in her chest as she thought of her move to Florida and how she wouldn't see Garrett and Molly and all her loved ones as frequently as she did now.

She sighed when she felt something cool and damp slide along her forehead. Her pulse skittered when she realized Garrett was stroking her face with a cool towel, and she felt out of breath as she murmured, "That feels good."

He dragged the damp cloth along her cheek, and the cool mist on her skin made her nipples bead under her T-shirt. His voice was low and sensually hypnotic. "So of all the states, why Florida?" He ran the towel along the length of her bare arms, and her nipples turned hard as stones.

With a delicious shiver, she sighed and leaned her cheek to her right, into his chest. "Some of my college friends live in Miami Beach. And I'm a sun person."

She hadn't realized she was grabbing onto his arm, but she knew that she didn't want to let go. He smelled so good and felt warm and substantial, so she kept her arms curled around his elbow. God, she'd done the impossible to get this man to notice her. The impossible. She'd dated men she hadn't even liked. She'd said she'd marry other men. Ignored Garrett and paid attention to everyone else. It had made him scowl, but that had been the whole extent of his reactions to her efforts.

It had been infuriating and disheartening.

He really did see her as some sort of friendly sister, while Kate had fantasized about him for decades. She hated that she never could really enjoy sex with her partners because a part of her heart had always belonged to this man.

This man who now caressed her neck with that cloth, and made her new purple panties damp with wanting. Even if she'd convinced herself she didn't love him anymore, her body was still hazardously attracted to his. Hell, if she weren't sick, she would open her eyes and kiss him even if he didn't want her to. She'd just go crazy and kiss him, because that was the only thing she'd never tried, of all the crazy stunts she'd pulled to get him to notice her. She had his attention with Florida. But this was no longer a stunt.

She had to leave. And she had to leave now.

So that when she came for a visit, she would have a new life, a steady boyfriend and an equally great catering business in Miami, and when she saw Garrett, she would see what she had been meant to see all along. A friend and a brother figure.

"Do you want me to bring my laptop here?" he whispered in her ear, his voice strangely husky. "Kate?"

She nodded, not opening her eyes as she released him and waited, with a new kind of fever, for him to come back.

Garrett was hard as granite and hated that he was, but he was trying his damnedest to ignore it as he set his laptop on the nightstand. He kept the computer shut, and instead kicked off his shoes and plopped down on the bed next to Kate, stretching his legs out as he put his arm around her shoulders, sensing her need for comfort.

She'd been holding his arm so hard, he hadn't wanted to move.

Hell, his back had gone stiff as a board as soon as her fingers had curled around him. He'd desperately wanted her touch and at the same time, he'd been distressed over the way his body responded to it. In the end, he'd wanted it more than he'd disliked it, and he'd come back. For more. Like a needy dog wanting a bone.

When she'd been getting dressed, he had thought he'd have a heart attack at the sight of that beautiful bare bottom. Kate was willowy and slim, and her wet hair had so temptingly caressed her shoulders. In a fraction of a second, he'd visualized about a dozen things he wanted to do to her, a dozen ways he wanted to kiss and feel her.

Now she was cuddling against his side, with that cute little T-shirt, and that soft, almost dreamlike smile on her lips.

He put his arm around her shoulders, and she sighed in contentment and snuggled into his chest, clutching a piece of his collar. The gesture was so possessive and sweet his chest knotted with emotion as he set his head back on the headboard and held her to him.

What would it be like to marry someone like Kate? Someone he cared for. He wanted. Not for any other purpose but because he needed her by his side.

Flooded with tenderness, he felt her squirm to get closer, and her T-shirt rode up to reveal…those purple panties that made his mouth water.

Just give me something to think about other than those long legs. Those sweet purple panties…

Her hair was still wrapped in a white towel, and Garrett gently unwound it and ran it slowly over her scalp, seeing her lashes resting on her cheekbones as she let him dry her hair, her skin pale in the sunlight.

He wanted to kiss those soft lips, which were natural and bare today, peachy in color. He wanted to slide his hands up her arms, touch her bare skin and memorize its texture, its color, its temperature. He wanted her eyelashes to flutter apart, so he could stare into her eyes and say something about the things roiling inside of him.

Instead, he finished drying her hair and tossed the towel onto the chair by the window. He shifted back to her side, noticing how she stiffened and tightened her hold on his collar until he wrapped his arm tightly around her again, and she relaxed.

He yanked off his tie and set it on the nightstand, and then wrapped his other arm around her waist and set his jaw on the top of her head. Her hair smelled of raspberries. He'd wanted to know? Yeah. He had his answer. And now his blood heated with one whiff. He grabbed the bed sheet and pulled it up over them both, not wanting her to notice his painfully pulsing erection if she opened her eyes.

She sighed and turned to him, snuggling closer. Her breasts brushed his ribs, and his body went crazy. He dragged his fingers down her shoulder and to her waist and stroked the little bit of skin exposed from her raised T-shirt.

He kissed her forehead. She didn't stir. Sweet baby, she looked so vulnerable today. He knew she was strong, but he still wanted to coddle her. He looked at her lips and ran a hand down her damp hair. He'd never wanted anything more than to make this woman happy. And right now, he wanted to kiss her.

"You awake, Kate?" he asked, his voice barely recognizable, it was so gruff.

She was breathing evenly, which confirmed she'd fallen asleep. Garrett slid his hand up and down her arm, his heart pounding. He bent his head and kissed her freckles, a light, dry kiss, and then he stole a kiss from her soft, marshmallow mouth.

Intoxicating. Soft. Female. *Perfect.*

Coming undone, he drank in her expression. Her eyes remained shut, her lashes forming titian-colored half-moons against her cheekbones.

He stroked the back of one finger down her jaw. She was everything he'd wanted and never allowed himself to have, and she was breathing like a baby, sleeping like one. He heard his own haggard exhale as he tried to draw back. He bent down again, softly brushing his lips over her forehead, then her nose, her cheekbones, her jaw…until he fitted his mouth back over her lips and whispered, "Kate."

She remained asleep, but sighed at her name and opened her mouth under his, her breath blending with his. Desire exploded in the pit of his stomach. The urge to splay his body over hers, open her lips wider, search her tongue with his, bury himself inside her, was so acute, he had to drag his jaw up her temple as he fought for control, completely infuriated with himself.

What was he doing?

Since when had he become a masochist?

He'd always known he couldn't have Kate. He'd done everything in his power to stay away from her. He'd hurt her enough, and he didn't truly feel he could ever make a woman happy when he had so many regrets on his shoulders.

It was hard to believe you were ever worthy when someone had died to give you your life.

But the thought of Kate leaving had set a beast loose inside him. He wanted to protect her and look after her, and just imagining that she could meet a man in Florida, a man she could have powerful feelings for, made him feel rabid to stake a claim.

Even now, when there were no states separating them and he was holding her snug in his arms, it just didn't seem like he could get close enough to her. He'd spent years pushing her away, and now it felt like she wouldn't ever let him back in.

And if she did, he didn't even know what he'd do with himself or this wanting.

Four

More than a week later, Kate's wood-paneled kitchen was a mess of cooking utensils as she, Beth and Molly fiddled around on the kitchen island. Kate and Beth had a looming deadline to cater a baby shower this afternoon. Worse, now only Beth would be going to set up, since Kate had had a last-minute change of plans.

Molly had been the one to deliver the plan-altering news less than an hour ago, when she'd casually mentioned that Julian had been asked to fill in for Garrett at the *San Antonio Daily* this morning. Garrett had come down with strep.

Kate had been floored. How could she not go and take care of him?

"You love that man like crazy, Kay. Just look at how you're running to his side at the first sign of trouble! I just can't see why you're so determined to leave Texas,"

Molly complained as she licked the remaining vanilla topping off a discarded spatula. Her cheek was smeared with a streak of red.

Since she was an artist, Kate's little sister always had smudges on her clothes, hair or face, but it only enhanced her bohemian style and made her look even cuter—especially to Julian, who would always tickle and poke her whenever she was "messy."

"You know, I thought you guys would bond over your strep throat," Molly continued with a frown. "You still could now that you gave it to him. Did he kiss you?"

Kate clicked the oven light on and peered through the window to check on Garrett's muffins. "Molly, please start supporting me a little more in my decision. I've told you I'll fly over here to see you as much as I can. We can talk on Skype all the time, too. And of course we didn't kiss. I'm not stupid! Who kisses a sick person?" Kate said in disgust.

"Someone who loves them."

She snorted. "We're not you and Julian."

"Kate, the day Julian and I got back together, he and Garrett had a talk. Julian tells me that the man is severely and painfully in love with you and doesn't even know it."

Kate's heart stuttered, and at that moment, her chest felt as spongy as the muffins she was watching through the oven window. She remembered the way Garrett had taken care of her the day she'd come home with strep.

He'd checked in on her every afternoon afterward, but that first day, he'd spent the night with her. A quiver raced down her skin when she remembered how they'd cuddled all night. He'd stayed dressed, like he had when he'd been drunk and crashed in her bedroom the night of his birthday, but he'd held her as if she was precious.

When she'd woken up in the middle of the night to realize he was holding her, she had been engulfed with such a feeling of happiness beyond what she'd ever felt before. On impulse, she'd stroked her fingers along his stubbled jaw, and he'd made a strange, groaning noise as he'd turned his face into her touch, his voice deliciously groggy. "You feel all right? Do you need anything?"

"Sorry. I'm perfect. Go to sleep."

She'd cuddled back down to hear his heart beat under her ear, and she'd wanted to stay awake just to memorize its rhythm. She'd never, ever, felt so whole. Which only made her feel sorry for herself now. Because they hadn't even kissed. Had he made her melt over some snuggles?

It wasn't just the snuggling. It was also that they'd known each other for so long they didn't even need to talk. When she'd woken up, he'd been awake and watching her with a smile on his handsome face, and his eyes had seemed to turn liquid as he'd run a finger down her cheek. "Fever's gone," he'd whispered.

And she'd almost swallowed her tongue and nodded. Because she'd known there was nothing she could do for the other kind of fever inside her. She'd had to remind herself that this was Garrett, a very stubborn, hardheaded Gage man, and that he wasn't her lover or a Prince Charming. Garrett had some serious baggage to deal with, and Kate had once loved him—too hard, and for too long, and too painfully—to allow so much as a little flicker of hope to linger.

Julian might think that Garrett had feelings for Kate, but all he surely felt was the same thing he'd always felt. Guilt and responsibility.

Beth spoke up from her corner of the island, where she busily worked her artistic skills on a tray of cookies for the shower. "You're shaking your head at me now, Kate, but now that I think about it, I also suspect Garrett has always had a thing for you."

"No, he doesn't. And I'm sick and tired of chasing after him like some tramp," Kate countered as she dumped the egg shells in the trash and wiped the granite counter clean.

Molly laughed. "Kate, you've never chased after Garrett, at least not blatantly. Men are sometimes stupid about those things—you need to be frank with them."

Frank?

All right, so let's be frank.

Kate had stripped in front of him. She had almost kissed him in her bed when he'd dragged that cool cloth around her body. Hell, she was pretty sure if she hadn't been sick, she would have thrown herself at him. And she'd done this with her plane ticket to Florida already sitting in her night drawer. That just couldn't be good. Could it?

She'd lain there with her eyes closed as he ran that cloth over her, and she'd been shaking in her bones as she'd imagined what it would feel like to be kissed by him. She'd even had dreams about it all during the week. Heat had spread through her at one particularly erotic one, when she'd felt him touch her aching nipples, then kiss them....

That night in her bed, she'd wanted to dissolve into his strong arms when he'd held her, and when he'd dried her hair, she'd been so affected and felt such desire pool between her thighs, she'd almost released an embarrassing sound that only her raw throat—abused by the strep—had been able to stop.

No. If she stayed here, she wouldn't be able to stay

away from Garrett, and seeing him while not having him would be torment. It had always been so, but after the night of his birthday, when he'd cradled her face and tried to tell her he'd do anything to fix her "dilemma," and after he'd nursed her when she was sick, it felt doubly so.

It.

Hurt.

The man might not love her as his mate, but he cared about her, and Kate knew this was exactly why she'd never be able to ever come clean with her feelings. He'd either feel awful about not responding, or feel pity for her and do something gallant like keep on sacrificing himself for her to make up for what he "took."

She. Had. To. Leave!

And start fresh, without Garrett's shadow tormenting and taunting her.

She knew it would be difficult. But she still had to leave. She had to give herself the chance, and Garrett his freedom.

Thinking about him, sick and bedridden today, made her stomach knot as she put on a floral-print oven mitt and bent over to pull the tray of muffins out of the oven. She'd made this particular recipe because it had lately become her favorite. The muffins were healthy and yummy, made of almond flour, with orange zest and black currants and walnuts. She set them on the cooling grill and prepared a small basket while the chicken soup finished.

"Food. That's how you guys make love, I swear. Those sounds he makes when he eats your cookies."

"Whoa!" Beth said from the corner, where she was now adding the decorations to the pacifier-shaped chocolate lollipops. "You're getting wicked, Molls!"

Molly laughed, fairly radiating mischief.

Beth laughed and shook her head, but then turned sober as she watched Kate stir the chicken soup. "Kate, it's not a bad idea. If you're taking that over to his apartment, you could totally seduce him. I mean, clearly the man wants you. Every time you're not looking, he's staring in your direction. Maybe if you guys work it out, you wouldn't be so determined to leave?"

"You're confusing him with Landon looking at you, Beth," Kate countered, turning off the stove. "Plus, I won't begin with the way Julian looks at you, Molly—oh, Lord, that man loves you."

"Does he?" Molly said with a cheeky grin, twirling the tip of her ponytail in one finger. "I don't ever tire of him telling me he does. God, I can't wait to marry him and make him all mine."

Looking thoughtful, Beth followed Kate to the cupboard as she pulled out a glass container.

"Kate, if Garrett didn't want you he wouldn't spend all day taking care of you when you look like leftovers."

Kate rolled her eyes. "Thanks, Beth. With friends like you, who needs an enemy?"

"Kate! Come on, listen to us. We're dishing out good advice here."

"Even if he *'wanted me'* for one crazy night and I managed to get him to drop his guard," Kate said, facing them, "I want love. If I can't have what you guys have, I'd rather be alone."

Molly sighed. For the first time since her Florida announcement, Kate could tell that the possibility of her moving to another state was truly sinking in. It hurt, too. To hurt them. She knew they didn't want her to leave, but she also knew that deep down, they understood.

"I still think you could find love here in Texas." Despite her words, Molly sounded more dejected now. "Garrett would make a *great* husband once he realizes everything that happened is *not his fault.*"

"Molly, please, I can't talk about this anymore. I don't love him anymore, and he's not interested in me. When will you guys understand? Garrett always gets what he wants. He's not a subtle man. If he wanted me, don't you think he'd go for me?"

When Beth and Molly exchanged sad looks and fell silent, Kate's stomach sank. Well, what had she expected? Had she wanted one of them to lie and contradict her? Maybe so, but the truth was the truth, and they couldn't change it.

Molly attempted to lighten up the suddenly somber ambience. "I still think it's sweet, you going over with soup and muffins."

"Well, he's obviously sick because of me. I have to repay the favor. I was thinking of doing something nice for him to say thank-you for taking care of me, anyway."

For holding me and watching my fever break and just making me feel like he cares at least a little bit.

Even if the devil's ultimate plan had probably been to remove Miami from Kate's agenda.

She sighed as she glanced at the muffins. Without further hesitation, she put them in a small basket, then poured the soup in a large glass container. This might be the last time in her life she nursed Garrett back to health, so she had to make it count.

The doorman recognized Kate as she walked into the marble lobby with her goodies in her arms. She told him that she was here to drop the stuff off for Garrett, and he allowed her to go up to the penthouse.

Trying not to make noise, she entered the palatial bachelor pad. It was simple and modern, with dark leather furniture with chrome accents, glass tables and dark walnut flooring. But what she most loved was the stainless-steel, state-of-the-art kitchen. It almost seemed to be merely decorative, since she knew Garrett rarely ate at home, but it was still worthy of a five-star restaurant.

Heating up the hot drawer, Kate slid the chicken soup container inside, and then set the muffins on a covered cake stand. Satisfied with her work, she resisted the urge to go primp herself, but did take a peek at her appearance in the mirror over the entry console.

She looked…quite nice, actually.

Now that she was no longer sick, the color had returned to her cheeks. Her eyes had a nice shine, as though she were excited about something, and the soft cotton sundress with blue-and-white stripes almost made it seem like she was ready for the beach. She'd bought it specifically with Florida in mind, but, oh well, today she'd felt like wearing something he hadn't seen her in before.

And she wasn't even going to dwell on her reasoning either.

It was only that he'd looked extra good when he'd come to see her and she'd felt and looked like crapola, and now she wanted him to…well, to think she looked like a fresh piece of sunshine.

"Garrett?" She called his name softly down the hall, her stomach turning leaden at each tentative footstep she took toward his bedroom. She didn't know what she'd do if she found him in bed with someone. Nothing, probably, but she would definitely cry about it later.

She knew he slept with women. A man like him had his choice of girls all the time. But Garrett had always been discreet about it and he'd never really paraded a lot of women in front of Kate. She couldn't begin to imagine how much it would hurt if she saw him kissing someone, or lying in bed with someone, or putting his arm around someone….

She paused at his open bedroom door, holding her breath. The drapes were wide open, letting the sun inside. His bedroom was done in different shades of gray and black, the nightstands made of ebony wood with chrome accessories. It was all so manly, she couldn't imagine any design more fitting to Garrett's dark good looks.

Something warm flitted through her when she spotted his prone figure on the bed. Her heart almost stopped when she realized he was only wearing a pair of black boxer briefs, the rest of his body covered in his natural golden tan and nothing else. Suddenly he looked very large, very dark and very powerful.

"Garrett?"

He stiffened almost imperceptibly, but Kate couldn't miss the tensing of the muscles in his back. "I'm going to kill my mother," he growled into his folded arm.

"She didn't tell me. Molly did."

"Then I'm going to kill Julian."

He rolled to his side and pulled the satiny gray bedspread up to his waist.

It was hard not to notice how beautiful his muscled torso was, and how sexy he looked with his dark hair all rumpled.

It was also hard not to notice his scowl.

Kate bit back a smile and stepped in with her arms up in feigned innocence. “Me. Come. In. Peace. Bring food. For. Grumpy. Man. May I pass?”

“Freckles, get away or you will get strep again.”

“I will not.”

“Get out of here, Katie.”

She shook her head. “Katie. No. Understand. What. Grumpy. Man. Says.”

“Grumpy man says *leave,*” Garrett said, but all of Kate’s maternal instincts had flared to life with just one look at him, and she couldn’t suppress the need to coddle this man like she had when they were younger and she’d helped Eleanor take care of him.

She kicked off her shoes, and before thinking about it, jumped onto the bed next to him, taking care not to touch any part of his body. “You’re not the only bed crasher, you know. I have full authority to crash your bed now that you’ve crashed mine twice.”

He sighed and closed his eyes, banging his head on the headboard. “Get out of my bed.”

“Not until you let me feed you. Starve the virus, feed the fever? Sound familiar? My part-time doc told it to me.”

“Docs are renowned for failing to take their own advice.”

“This one is special. Hey, have they medicated you?”

“I’m already drugged as hell. I don’t want to eat, Freckles. Just get out of here.”

Now Kate scowled, too.

“Garrett, why won’t you look at me? Are you in pain? You look like you are.”

“Yeah, I’m in pain.”

"What is it? Is it your head?" She felt his forehead and he was definitely hot. And she noticed he'd stiffened.

"Don't," he murmured, seizing her wrist and returning her hand to her lap.

Eyes widening at the lines of agony carved in his face, she curled her fingers into her palm because they tingled after his touch.

He inhaled long and deep before his lids finally lifted open, and her heart melted when he looked at her with that dark, tired gaze. His glassy look killed her, but something there, something she couldn't decipher, made her stomach constrict. His pupils were fully dilated and his eyes held a strange awareness.

"Please just leave," he said, and there was something very desperate in his voice that almost made her hesitate.

"Come here, Garrett." She slid closer until her back was against the gray suede headboard, and she urged his dark head to rest against her chest and ran her fingers through his hair. "If you don't want to eat, just let me keep you company."

He groaned on contact, and wrapped his arms around her waist. "Kate, I don't have the energy to do this with you today."

"This what? I'm not planning to fight you."

"This… Damn." He made another deep noise when she lightly massaged his scalp. As her fingers twined in his hair and he pressed closer and tightened his hold around her, her body experienced all sorts of chemical reactions. He was adorable. She wanted to hug him. To tuck him into her suitcase and take him with her.

Crazy girl. The point was to get away from him, wasn't it?

She continued caressing his hair until he relaxed

against her, and her body also turned mushy. When his voice reached her ears minutes later, she started, for she'd almost been falling asleep with him.

"You used to bring me soup when I was sick." He spoke in a murmur against her chest, and his warm breath slipped seductively into her cleavage. "I liked getting sick because of you."

She laughed. "You're a very troubled man, Garrett."

"I was a very troubled young boy."

He angled his face so he could peer up at her, then raised his hand and absently ran his thumb down the bridge of her nose. "And you? You weren't Little Miss Perfect. When you heard the thunder and lightning and that huge storm one night, you lost your marbles completely. Do you remember?"

She dropped her hands as he sat up.

"I'm not sure, since I lose my marbles with all the storms."

"The one that made both you girls run into the boys' room. Before we knew it, Molly had jumped into Julian's bed and you were in mine. But Jules tried to hide her under the covers, and you and I immediately went all around the house looking for Molly, thinking she was somewhere else."

"Okay. Now I remember."

He sat back with his temple propped against the headboard, his eyes suddenly warm with the memory. "You and I ended up splitting up to find Molly, and I found you asleep in the living room after I found out Julian had hijacked her and was hiding her in his bed. Do you remember what you said?"

Kate was so riveted by his retelling, by the way his

smile flashed as he remembered, she'd lost all power of speech. He looked…happy. And also sad?

And devastating.

When she didn't answer, he tipped her head back by the chin, and his voice acquired a strange note. It was deeper. Especially with that strep-throat rasp. "You asked me why I hadn't hijacked you, too."

A strange tingle was growing in the pit of Kate's stomach, and she couldn't stop it, couldn't control it.

"I was probably more asleep than awake."

The atmosphere around them felt heavy with something unnameable and untamable. She became fiercely aware of every point of contact of their bodies. Her knee against his thigh. Her shoulder against the side of his arm.

"Do you want me to hijack you now, Kate?"

Her stomach tightened at the question. "What do you mean?" She narrowed her eyes and told herself his husky tone was due to the strep throat, but it was too thick, too heavy, as heavy as those coal-black eyes.

He cupped her cheek in one huge, dry palm. "You always took care of Molly until she found Julian. You always put her first, before anything else. Didn't you?"

When Kate could only nod, he continued.

"This is how I am with you, Kate. It's instinctive in me. Putting you first. I'd never take advantage of you, that's my number-one priority. But if I knew you might want something from me, I would like to give it to you. So…"

Suddenly he looked as hungry as he did when he ate her food.

"Do you want me to hijack you?" he asked. "Want

me to come after you? Is that why you're leaving for Florida? Do you want me to give chase?"

His stare was so piercing and primal, he didn't look weak or sick at all.

He looked predatory and male, and she felt fragile and female. Inside her, a dozen words rippled with the need to come forth.

I want you. Please give me your love. Yourself.

But how could she tie him up this way? Was this really the answer he wanted? Or was he seeking for her to appease him by saying that she didn't need anything else from him? He'd given her so much already. For his whole life.

A sound of protest tore from her chest, and it sounded so sexual, Kate swallowed it back in horror.

He smiled slowly, almost seductively, as his thumb trailed down the curve of her jaw. "Cat got your tongue?"

Kate couldn't think. Speak. Breathe.

His thumb went lower, and now slowly brushed over the sleeve of her dress. Then it trailed down her bare arm, the touch a shivery, silken whisper that made her insides quiver with yearning. Her heart galloped as pure need kicked in. His other fingers joined his thumb to caress the inside of her left arm, and her skin broke out in goose bumps as her lungs strained for air.

Garrett was quiet as he watched her reactions. She realized she hadn't pulled away from his touch, but instead had leaned closer.

He slid the fingers of his other hand into her hair, softly tangling them inside the loose mass. He watched her with somber expectation, as though wondering if she would stop him.

She didn't.

Oh, why didn't she?

What on earth was he doing?

What was she doing?

Intense sexual thoughts began to flicker through her mind. Garrett's lips, his beautiful body naked against hers…

Their gazes held, both of them silent, their eyes almost questioning but also on fire with desire. His breath, slow and deep and slightly uneven, bathed her face.

Suddenly, he tugged her dress up her thighs and then slid his hand under the fabric, up her panty-clad bottom, then up her back, his fingers slowly tracing the little dents of her spine.

Kate sucked in a mouthful of air.

She probably should stop him. She probably should. Instead, she trembled and bent to brush a kiss across his lightly stubbled jaw. Then she drew back and noticed that his eyes were closed, his face almost in an expression of pain. She cupped his jaw and kissed his forehead, her insides melting when he groaned, encouraging her, so that she kissed the tip of his nose.

His hands were suddenly on her hips. Pushing her away? No. He drew her over his lap, guiding her so that she straddled him, and suddenly his fingers stole under her panties to caress her buttocks as his nose slid down the length of hers. She should pull away, but she was breathless, waiting for something, anything, as he buzzed her lips with his. "Kate, stop me," he said softly.

Five

Holy hell, what was he doing?

He blamed the seven freckles on her nose. They made him do stupid stuff.

He blamed the strep, the fact that he was on steroids, antibiotics and some strange tea his mother had made him this morning. He blamed the fact that Kate smelled like spring and raspberries. He'd never been so hungry, and he didn't know if a thousand men could tear her away from his arms today.

He was fixated on her lips. It was surreal, so surreal, having Kate in his bed. "Stop me, Katie," he found himself saying, as he continued to run his hands up and down her thighs, and grip her lovely bottom.

He wanted to squeeze her so tight he feared he'd break her bones. He shouldn't be touching her buttocks, but he was too tired to fight the urge and too sick to care. They felt too good. *She* felt too good.

He'd wanted to do this since he'd seen her slide into those purple panties and he'd been haunted ever since. Why had she done that little striptease? He couldn't stop thinking she'd wanted him to see her. She'd wanted him to want her.

And he did, he really did.

"You think I'm blind? That I don't know?" he murmured against the top of her head. He drew back and stared into her face, noticing how soft her lips looked parted. "What you want is right here—and you'll want it whether you're in this room with me or all the way in Florida. You'll want *me*."

He didn't know why he was testing her like this. But he wanted to see…

If she feels anything for me.

Anything even remotely resembling this madness that I feel.

He caught her closer when she squirmed and tried to push herself away. "You have no idea what I want!" she angrily spat.

"I know exactly what you want! I notice it every time you look at me, like I'm everything you've ever wanted. But I'm not, Kate. We both know I'm not. There's not a day I don't remember what I took from you—"

"Shut up, Garrett! You're sick and…medicated and clearly out of your mind."

He caught her back against him and stroked her cheeks as tenderly as he could, but knew his hands were shaking. "I know you'll probably hate me for this, but I still won't let you go to Florida. I want you close to me, where I know you're safe."

"I'm not asking for your permission!"

He frowned and stared into her beautiful shining eyes, wondering why he couldn't have this girl, why he felt like he was poison for this girl.

"So you'll make me follow you? Hmm? Is that what you want, Kate?"

She glared at him, and he couldn't stand that little glarc. Hc sct a kiss on her forehead and rubbed her back under her dress, and she shuddered and pressed closer. Her need seeped into him, warming him to the core, until he felt like a torch was blazing inside of him. Blazing for her. He could feel her need of him like you'd feel rain pelting your back or the sun on your face. There were days when he could successfully ignore the pull between them, the undeniable chemistry. But tonight, his heart beat like a crazed drum for her. His muscles strained with aching desire. He could hardly stand not to touch her, felt dizzy with temptation, weak from fighting it.

"Do me a favor and say you'll stay?" He nuzzled her face with his own. "Stay with your family. With me."

His chest cramped as he thought about what he felt for her. What he felt for Kate was like a storm, and it was always there, consuming him from the inside, tormenting his every living moment.

Her voice sounded resentful. "Why? So I can keep on playing my Oscar-worthy role of the good little—"

He lost it. It was the anger and need in her voice, the closeness of her body. It was Kate. Driving him past the point of obsession, past the point of reason. He curled his hands around the back of her head and growled, "Damn you, the only one playing thc rolc of a frcaking wallflower, pretending not to want you like this, is *me,*" and his mouth pressed, scorching and hungry, against hers.

He hadn't meant to kiss her. He hadn't planned to crush her body against his and part her lips with his own. He hadn't planned to hungrily push his tongue into her soft mouth, but he did all that, because he needed to. And when she responded by twining her arms around his neck and releasing a soft moan that nearly drove him to his knees, he did more.

He wanted her, wanted her more than air, more than food, water, anything.

Blood boiling in his veins, he grabbed her curvy buttocks and molded her body tighter against his as he twirled his tongue around hers, wildly tasting every inch of her warm, giving mouth. The kiss was fire, lightning, electrifying to him, surpassing his every dream and fantasy about her. Surpassing any other kiss he'd ever had.

He was thirty already, and he had never felt so out of control, gotten so carried away with a woman before. His arms, his legs, his every muscle shook uncontrollably with pure, raw lust, as if one mere taste of Kate alone was enough to make him addicted to her. And he was, he *was* addicted.

Her luscious flavor, the erotic little moans she poured into his mouth, stimulated his thirst to levels far beyond quenching. He wanted her so much he could eat her up alive and still not be satiated. He could lick every inch of her creamy skin and be still ravenous for more. Because she was everything he wanted and everything he couldn't have. *Dammit.*

It took an inhuman effort for him to draw back, and he did it with a pained sound from deep within his throat.

"Kate, do you know what's happening here?" He

panted hard for his breath, and dropped his head, unable to resist her.

His hungry mouth opened wide around the fabric of her dress and he sucked hard, mindlessly, as his hand cupped her breast from beneath and squeezed the tip even farther out for him to suck.

"Garrett," she gasped as he drew her nipple, fabric and all, deeper into his mouth.

He groaned in ecstasy, turning his head to nuzzle the tip of her second breast. "Kate, if you don't want this—stop me…stop me now…."

She palmed his jaw and drew his mouth up to hers, searing him with her eager kiss, her lips trembling with desire.

He groaned and shut his eyes when she dragged her mouth up to kiss his nose, then his eyelids, and an out-of-control shudder wracked his large body.

He knew he was losing himself in the fragrant scent of her arousal, in the feel of her small body trembling against his, in the sound of tears in her voice. He should make her leave, so he could go back to hell. But some demon was shouting at him that he was losing her, that she would be out of his life in weeks, and suddenly he couldn't take it.

"Three seconds," he rasped as he opened his eyes, his hands unsteady as he cupped her breasts and used his thumbs to circle the budded peaks. "You have three seconds to tell me to stop."

To emphasize his words, he gave her another branding kiss, praying that she would resist him.

And that somebody would just whack his head from behind, tie up his hands and gag his mouth, so that he didn't use them all over her body like he was aching to.

Because he just couldn't withhold his desire any longer. He didn't care if he was going to hell. As far as he was concerned, he'd been living there for years, and every one of those years, he'd wanted her.

Yeah, he must be a devil to be here with this angel in bed, ready to have the best sex of his life with her. Ready to make the fantasies he'd had for hours and days and weeks and months and years come true for him. For both of them.

I'm going to hell and it will damn well be worth it....

"One," he warned.

Kate only watched him, as though waiting for him to get to three to kiss him again. The thought made him grind out, "Two."

She looked thoroughly kissed and ready to be taken. He'd never in his life wanted anything so much.

"Three."

When she sighed in outward relief and never made so much as a move to stop him, he went crazy. He pulled her dress over her head and tossed it to the floor, then trailed his lips down her flushed face as his hands coasted down the sides of his newly revealed treasure. She was smooth, slim and curvy, and she made him want to kneel at her feet and revere her. Adore her. Make love to her until they died from it.

With a little sound of frustration, Kate reached to the waistband of his underwear and tugged down his boxer briefs.

He helped her, and once he was naked, rolled around immediately, almost crushing her with his weight as he flattened her back on the bed and held her by the hair. His tongue plunged into her mouth, flooding him with her essence, feeding his reckless thirst.

Her bare skin slid against his as she suckled his tongue, and the unexpected act triggered ripples of pleasure through his system. She rubbed her breasts against his chest while he slanted his head for deeper access to her. Crazy good. She tasted crazy, crazy good.

Warnings shot across his mind as he pulled open her bra. This was the time to stop, but he was past stopping.

He did not care about anything else except branding her, taking her to a place where there would be no talk of Florida, no talk of leaving; there would be nothing but the two of them. Together.

He shoved the fabric aside and exposed her nipples. Perfect and pink.

He cupped one in his big hand and licked his way down her throat, down to the pebbled nipple. He groaned at her taste, then slid his fingers between her parted thighs and easily yanked down her panties. Squirming restlessly, she pulled him up by the hair, to her lips, and kissed him while she breathlessly murmured, "Hurry."

He cradled her head and angled her back for his devouring kiss. Murmuring her name softly, he blanketed her body with his, his erection nestling between her legs.

He ducked his head to nibble hungrily on her lips and reached between her legs again, stroking his fingers along her slick folds. She was so hot and wet. He groaned, then stuck his finger into her channel only to bring it up and stick that finger into his mouth, tasting her before he stroked and penetrated her again. "How long has it been for you?" he asked, her tightness closing around him.

"A long time," she gasped.

"How long?" he pressed.

"Years."

He closed his eyes as his chest swelled with emotion. *Mine, mine, mine,* he thought, noting how tight she was, how hot she was, as she rocked her hips to his caress.

The fact that she had also not been with anyone for a long time made him wild. He already felt dangerously close to orgasm as he added his thumb to caress her tender spot. He watched her toss and turn in pleasure, his erection throbbing painfully between his legs.

She's going to be just yours from now on....

He couldn't think beyond sinking himself inside her, taking something no one would ever take from her. Her sex was slick against his fingers as she curled her legs around him and locked her ankles at the small of his back, urging him on with a sensual rock and a breathless, "Please. Garrett, please, I hurt."

She wants me so much she's hurting for me....

Groaning softly out of pure sheer overwhelming need, he slid his hands up her arms and intertwined their fingers as he pinned her hands at her sides.

"Are you ready, Katie?"

Her voice got strangled in her throat, thick with need and desire. "Please, yes."

His body tensed in anticipation as he teased his hardness along her entrance. She was slick and wet and swollen—so damned perfect. He closed his eyes and savored her body as he gently prodded her entry, inch by inch, slow and deep, releasing a growl of pure animal need. "Ahh, Kate."

"Garrett," she cried out and stiffened. A killer wave of red-hot ecstasy whipped through him, tensing his muscles that already strained for release.

He groaned when he realized he wasn't wearing any protection.

"Kate…damn…"

She cried out when he dragged out, grabbing his shoulders and saying, "Don't stop, don't stop!"

He groaned in torment and eased back in, totally lost in her heat. The sound she released was slow and dark, as if the pain were morphing into pleasure. "Better?" he rasped.

He took her answering whimper in his mouth and kissed deeper until her body was writhing wildly underneath his.

He drove inside her once more.

Kate gasped, moaning out his name, and it was the sexiest thing he'd ever heard her say. And when she said, "More," he snapped and began a frantic pace.

They kissed like crazy for several minutes, and then she clutched his hard shoulders and gazed up at him with cloudy blue eyes.

She was so damned beautiful like this—this was how he wanted to have her every night in his bed. Red hair. Coral lips. Rosy cheeks. Thickened, recently kissed nipples.

He didn't even remember that his body hurt, that his throat was raw. All he knew was that Kate watched him, her breath rippling from between his lips as they moved together. All he knew was that he was shattering with pleasure as he gripped her waist and increased the pace. He thrust deeper, harder, lost in her grip, her heat, in *her.*

A knot of ecstasy pulled inside him and shot him off to outer space, and with three more thrusts, he pushed her past the precipice into an explosion that made her shout his name as he sank all the way home, spilling himself inside her.

For minutes they lay there, entangled and sweaty. He was breathless, sated and frankly, awed as hell.

He'd never felt so whole. He'd never made love like this. He shifted to look at her, then groaned at the sight of her languid body and dewy face, so beautiful and so taken.

"I'm sorry I lost control, Katie," he murmured, kissing her cheek, loving how warm and loose she felt as she snuggled closer. "I should've worn protection. What day are you in your cycle?"

"I don't know. Eight maybe," she said, tucking her face in his neck, as if hiding from his prying eyes. "Please don't worry, Garrett."

"Eight. Is that even safe…?" Man. He'd been as careless and excited as an adolescent to touch her. Not using protection had been inexcusable, made his chest churn with disgust at himself. "Freckles, damn…"

She sat up and pushed his hands away, shaking her head. "Please just…please stop apologizing for it, Garrett. I wanted this to happen, so did you. We had fun, it was great, it's done. There's no need to get all serious about it, and there's certainly no need for you to add it to your guilt bag."

Garrett sat back, so stunned at her words, his mind came up blank. Guilt bag? So she thought he had a guilt bag?

"What the hell is that supposed to mean?" he demanded.

"It means it was no big deal! It was just sex. You've had it with millions of women and I plan to do the same with other men in the future. I don't want you to apologize and I definitely don't want you considering…thinking that it could possibly…everything is all right here, okay?"

"I'm trying to be responsible. If there are repercussions—"

"Stop! Just stop! Even if there *were*..."

"If there were, I need to fricking *know* before I enter into any sort of agreement with Cassandra Clarks!" he angrily barked.

Kate stiffened. "What do you mean? What agreement?"

His lips formed a thin, angry line.

"What agreement, Garrett?"

He groaned and raked a hand through his hair, then let his hand fall. "She wants to marry me as a condition for selling us her share of Clarks."

"Marry…*you?*"

A thousand expressions crossed her face, until hurt ended up on the forefront, and Garrett felt like an ass.

"You! How dare you touch me when you're thinking of…I would *never* marry for anything other than love!"

He winced as she angrily jumped out of bed and searched for her dress.

He'd just had sex without a condom and honestly? He didn't even care.

He wanted her. He just wanted her. If it meant taking responsibility and doing something about it now, he would. But now it felt like the last thing she wanted was to be tied to him.

She'd basically told him that she thought the worst of him, that she wouldn't marry him if he were the last man on earth. Of course she didn't want him. He'd mucked up her entire life, and if she got pregnant, he'd muck it up again, taking her dream of Florida away from her.

The realization hurt him so much, he could only watch her from the bed, wondering if he'd actually stayed away from her all these years out of duty, or because he was a coward and knew, deep down, that he just didn't deserve her.

"Do you want some of the food I brought over, or should I just go home now?" she asked, and as if she'd already decided on the latter, she slipped back into her dress. Then she resumed searching on the floor for her panties.

He held them out to her with a scowl. "You were trembling in this bed with me, Kate. You. *Begged.* For me."

"You're right." She covered her face with shaking hands, then plunged her legs into her panties. "I even started it."

He was baffled. She looked very perturbed by the fact that she'd slept with him. He didn't know what to make of it when he'd just felt her writhe beneath him, wet and wanton.

"No. *I* did, Kate. I started it," he said, gentling his voice, standing up to embrace her. "Hell, I've been thinking about doing this with you since…"

Her eyes widened as though he'd just divulged something completely damning. "Since when? Since I said I was going to Florida? Ohmigod, are you trying to use sex to get me to bend to your will and stay here? Why else would you touch me when you haven't your whole life!"

She suddenly looked enlightened, while he stared blankly at her, puzzled and confused. Her cheeks were reddening by the second, but Garrett was growing too angry at her accusation to care. "Kate, do you seriously believe I'm that cold and calculating?"

Did she think anything even remotely redeeming about him, and was there any chance in hell she could ever love him when she was holding their past against him?

"Of course I do! You're a man who just confessed to be considering some sort of weird business marriage with some bimbo you barely even know!"

"She's not a bimbo, Kate," he said, just to be fair to Cassandra.

Kate's cheeks went redder. "You still haven't told me why you went behind your beloved's back and slept with me."

"Why don't you first tell me why the hell you slept with *me?* Were you just horny or did you just pity me tonight, or were you apologizing for giving me strep?"

"Who do you think you are to judge? Garrett, you *slept* with me even while thinking of marrying some stranger in the name of...business. I swear that's the most disgusting thing anyone's ever done to me!"

"You're just goddamned playing with me! You've teased me your whole life, parading around with other men! You just gave me a little taste of what I want, and once you got what you wanted, you're ditching me!"

She glared and stomped to the door. "Go to hell!"

"I'm already there, Kate. It's been my damned zip code since I was ten!"

As she stormed out of the room and slammed the door behind her, Garrett punched his fist into the pillow and yelled, "Goddammit!"

Six

"We're sitting at twenty-eight percent today…" Landon said. As usual, the man droned on and on about business.

Garrett made it a point to occasionally nod as if he were listening while he scrolled through his last text conversation with Kate. He'd texted her in the middle of the night after the debacle of their argument four nights ago. He'd been lying awake at midnight feeling medicated and as low as a dog. All he'd needed was for someone to put a bowl of Alpo out for him. Instead he'd found her food in the kitchen, cursed himself over and over again, heated up his soup and chowed down on several muffins, then grabbed his phone and texted her. Despite the fact that it had been past one in the morning, she'd replied. Which meant she'd been lying awake, too, as sleepless as he was.

Thanks for my food. When can I see you? I want to talk.

Everything is fine. I've already forgotten about it.

Garrett wasn't so stupid as to believe this, but had answered.

K. So I hear you're getting your dresses fitted Wednesday. I'll drive you.

Won't your girlfriend get jealous?

I'd like to explain to you about her.

It's fine. The fitting is at five so I'll see you before then.

"Are you even listening, Garrett?"

He lifted his head to Landon's confused gray gaze. "Hmm? What?"

Landon scowled and then continued, raising his voice as though to be clearer. "Clarks…new strategy…"

So, Kate thought Garrett had planned it all?

How could she believe that he'd planned to get sick, so that he could get her to bring over some food for him, get her into bed, seduce her like some out-of-control adolescent and conveniently forget a condom so she might have to stay? Well, hell, it sounded so brilliant, he felt like an idiot for not thinking of it before.

"Garrett, dammit, did you hear?"

"Yes. Clarks. A new strategy." He set his phone aside, but putting thoughts about Kate aside wasn't that easy.

"You're the last single Gage. Will you or won't you go through with this?" Landon asked.

With a major wrench of mental muscles, Garrett

pulled his scrambled brain together and tried to focus on the topic today.

"All three of us know that I'm not really the last single Gage, Lan." Garrett leaned back to survey both his brothers' expressions across the conference table.

Landon's eyebrows shot up. "Don't go there."

"Why not?" He shrugged. "He's still a Gage."

"Mother wanted nothing to do with him. Hell, we paid him millions to get out of our lives for good, and you want to bring him back?"

"How badly do you want Clarks?" Garrett countered.

"As badly as you want it," Landon returned.

Garrett scraped a hand along the tense muscles at the back of his neck. He wanted Clarks, but not as bad as he wanted something else.

"Plus who's to say that selfish bastard will want to help us?" Landon rose to pace by the wall of windows. "He will want a big piece of the pie, and he'll want even more than that. Do you remember Father refused to recognize him?"

"But we know he was Father's son, no matter how many times he denied it to Mother," Garrett countered. He'd been wracking his brain for other options and this was, fortunately or unfortunately, the only one he'd been able to come with.

To bring their illegitimate half brother, Emerson Wells, back into the fold.

Julian chewed on the back of a pen before he lowered it and spoke. "We could entice him with money. Stock. Something. Maybe we should call just him."

"He's trouble," Landon said pointedly, his face furrowed in thought. "What does he do now anyway?"

"Last I heard he was in the personal security business here in San Antonio. Started as a bodyguard."

"Seriously?"

"What can I say? He likes beating people up."

"All right then." Crossing the room, Landon clicked the phone intercom and rang his assistant. "If you'd please get me Emerson Wells on the line. You should be able to do a Google search and find his number. He owns some sort of personal security business here in town."

Hanging up, Landon rubbed his chin thoughtfully, his gray eyes on Garrett. "If he denies us…would you still go through with it?"

Kate's face and words surfaced in his mind with a vengeance, and his chest cramped. *I would never marry for anything other than love!*

For one painful moment, he wondered if she'd even care whether he married someone else, for whatever reason. But although her words had cut through him, her body had spoken another language. He'd lost control, and so had she. They'd both been so needy he hadn't even been able to stop to put on a condom.

What had he done?

Perhaps Garrett hadn't technically broken his promise to her father, but he felt like he had. There was probably no man more undeserving of Kate's affection than he.

Clearly, you blew it, Gage.

But she had wanted him. Hell, she'd not only wanted him, she'd melted under his touch. Was he supposed to turn his mind blank and forget about a moment like that?

"Molls said they have a fitting this afternoon that you insisted on driving them to?"

He glanced up at Julian in confusion. "Molly? I told Kate I'd drive her. I didn't know it included Molly."

"And Beth," Landon added with a grin. "They're all going together."

Garrett almost groaned. So much for talking to Kate one-on-one.

"Fine, then. I'll drive the three of them," Garrett reluctantly conceded. An infuriating hunch told him that Kate was doing this on purpose. Clearly, she had no desire to discuss anything with him.

Julian dropped his pencil on the table and angled his head, his eyes sparkling in amusement.

"You know, bro, I can't help you here. Molls would strangle me if I see her in *the* dress."

"That's fine." He plunged a hand through his hair. He'd wanted to spend some time with Kate and talk, but he would manage somehow. "I'll drop Kate off last and see if she'll do dinner with me."

"So I take it this means whatever Emerson says, you're not keen on the marriage of convenience?" Julian queried.

"Would you be?" Garrett countered. "Keen to marry a stranger? When your every thought is consumed by someone else?"

"Why don't you just tell Kate how you feel and get it all out there?"

Garrett shook his head.

Because he didn't deserve her.

Hell, the way things stood, even if he were to tell Kate how she made him feel, she'd probably tell him to stick his declaration where it hurts. She resented him for having taken her father from her, no matter how much she tried to pretend she didn't. He still couldn't forget those words she'd lashed out at him with when they were young: *How dare you!*

He'd never forget the hurt betrayal in her eyes when she'd found out her father had died because Garrett hadn't run as he'd been told to. And now, to top it off, she believed he'd deliberately slept with her just to make sure she stayed in San Antonio. True, it might have been the catalyst, but that was so not the reason.

"You know, Garrett," Landon said, coming over to pat his back, "we all get the love we think we deserve…and you *deserve* it, man. No matter what you think. You both do. So you better own it before she leaves for Florida, brother. Neither Julian nor I, nor for that matter, Mother, has any desire to watch what her departure does to you."

Seven

Kate checked herself in the mirror for the tenth time. She wore a plain khaki skirt and sleeveless halter top. She knew that it would be silly to try on another top, so she grabbed her purse and her phone, then glanced down on impulse at Garrett's last texts.

He'd said he wanted to talk and tell her about the "bimbo," but just thinking about the way he'd defended her made Kate's blood boil. Worse was that every time she went back a little further, to his kisses, little bubbles of remembrance shot through her system. She didn't want the bubbles. Or the tingles. Or any of the gut-churning jealousy she felt when she thought about him and Cassandra Clarks.

She hadn't slept a wink last night; she could still feel his touch on her traitorously sensitive skin. Now, Beth and Molly were waiting in her living room for him to pick them up, and Kate was grateful for the buffer they would provide.

Coward. That's why you asked them to come over.

Yes, yes, so fine, she was a coward. She just didn't trust herself to be alone with him. She feared she'd either do something sexual, which she had to put a stop to, or say some other cruel things that she didn't mean. She regretted getting so defensive when he'd started apologizing. Garrett was actually the most unselfish man she knew. He'd always thought ahead to how he would protect her if something unexpected happened. But the last thing Kate had wanted was to add to his burdens when it came to her. She hadn't ever imagined they'd end up naked and entangled. But he'd been there. So available. So sexy, tan and bare-chested. How could she resist? And the bastard had broken remorselessly through her walls, all in his stupid attempt to bend her to his will and liking!

But then he'd pretended to be hurt by her accusation, and accused her of being a tease. The reminder made her frown. She'd never considered that she was. Did she tease him? She'd tried to make him jealous for years, but she'd never known it had even had an effect.

Maybe it had more than he'd let on.

"Landon thinks he's going to do it," Beth was telling Molly.

"Do what?" Kate asked as she came back into the living room.

Molly turned to her with a sad, moping face. "Marry Cassandra Clarks. Jules told me yesterday. I just didn't know how to bring it up."

Kate's stomach clenched.

"It's got something to do with acquiring Clarks Communications," Beth said, shaking her head. "Kate, I'm sorry."

Once again, Kate felt the painful stab of jealousy inside her. "All the more reason I should leave," she whispered.

"You'd let the man you love marry another woman?" Beth asked uncertainly.

"If he wants her, yes. And I don't love him. I might have had a crush, but I'm over that. I'm in love with the idea of Florida now."

"Kate, I think it's hard for him to let himself want something, with what happened to your father, but I've always seen that he's got it bad for you," Beth said.

"No. *I* had it bad for *him*. And now I've promised myself to forget him. I should find a man with no baggage who actually makes me feel loved, Beth."

Both women quietly watched her pace to the window and then back.

"So there's nothing going on between the two of you? The boys say he's distracted. And so are you," Beth insisted.

Her best friend's eyes twinkled all of a sudden, and Kate wanted to groan when she saw Molly's mischievous smile also appear. Did they suspect Kate had totally gone sex-crazed at Garrett's place several days ago?

"There's nothing going on. We're…normal. Friends." *Who slipped up once,* she mentally added. Through the window, she watched his silver Audi pull over to the curb. Little bugs tickled the insides of her stomach. "He's here."

"I guess I'll just slide into the back with Molly," Beth offered as they went outside, and Kate locked up behind her.

She hated how her heart pounded when she walked up to the shiny silver car. Garrett stood holding the door open, his eyes sweet and liquid chocolate as he smiled. "Hi, Katie."

Her bones went mushy every time he called her Katie. "Hey, Garrett." His broad shoulder brushed hers as she got in, and her pulse sped with his nearness as he bent to kiss her on the cheek.

Oh, God, please don't be nice today, she thought miserably.

She could handle fighting with him. But this?

The thought of him marrying anyone, touching anyone like he'd touched her, tortured her.

He settled behind the steering wheel. She watched his hands on the gearshift as they sped off, and her core warmed and boiled hot as she remembered the ways he'd caressed her. Every part of her body wanted to do it again except her mind, where warning bells were ringing at full volume.

She couldn't let it happen again.

He was talking *marriage* to another woman.

She was only too glad she wouldn't be here to watch it.

After forty-five minutes at the dress shop, Garrett could now totally understand his brothers' amused grins from only hours ago.

He'd never gone to a dress fitting before.

Torture.

He sat on a chair outside a line of dressing rooms and watched as the ladies came out to stand before a huge mirror, where a busy little woman picked and poked and stabbed the material until she'd shaped it to her liking.

He'd been doing fine, answering emails on his iPhone, until Kate came out and took his breath away.

He watched her hop onto the platform and model the dress, exposing her slim, creamy ankles as she discussed the length with the short, busy-bee shop attendant. He felt as if a grenade had just exploded in his chest. His blood heated as he remembered the hell of watching her grow up, grow breasts, wear her hair longer, develop those curves. He'd seen her in her prom dress, in a barely there black bikini that hugged her silken curves in all the right places and made Garrett hurt in all the wrong ones.

He'd seen her naked in his bed…writhing in his arms….

And once he got her back there, he never wanted to see her dressed again.

He wanted to touch her, hold her.

He wanted to hear her breathe next to him at night. He just knew if she slept at his side, the mere feel of her would make all his nightmares vanish.

He suddenly saw, clearly, how he'd be complete and whole with her. How he'd feel worthy and needed in a way he had never, ever felt before. But at the same time, he'd be vulnerable. Because, holy God, he needed this woman so much.

He saw her eyes go bright when the girls came over, squealing in delight.

"That blue looks so good on you," Molly gushed.

"Oh, your date is going to be so thrilled!"

Garrett cocked a brow as he pushed himself off the chair and came over, listening to her ask if they were sure.

He stood next to her and caught her gaze in the mirror. "Date?"

She spun around to face him and her lips trembled in a smile. "I don't know. We won't be catering so I'll have some time to spare."

"Exactly. Flirt around with a man. Have a little fun," Molly said from nearby. Garrett couldn't miss the mischievous glint in Molly's eyes as she surveyed Garrett for a reaction.

He gave her none.

"Do we want this fitted…?" The saleslady maneuvered Kate's skirt, and Garrett watched in rapture as the woman tucked the fabric around her waist to enhance Kate's luscious curves even more.

He studied her breasts, how lush they were, tightly constrained by the corsetlike bodice. His mouth watered and his hands ached. He was in hell and heaven at the same time, and it was the most puzzling feeling he'd ever experienced.

Kate stared at his reflection, her blue eyes shining in concern and somehow pleading for a compliment. "Do you like it?"

They both stared at one another, and for that one moment, nothing mattered but her. She held his gaze, and he held hers. His world centered around this one woman he'd always tried not to want.

His eyes trailed along her body, taking her in, and he heard the soft, amusing sound of her breath catching. The gown was sapphire-colored, consisting of a tight corset top clinging to her body like second skin, then flaring into a wide skirt. He wanted to toss it up in the air and bury himself between her legs. Her arms were toned and slim, her breasts perky and tightly constricted, making him want to free them. Her glossy hair, too long and beautiful to keep restrained, hung down her shoulders.

She was gazing at him nervously, wetting her lips. "Garrett…do you like it?" she repeated.

He nodded while his body burned under his skin.

Smiling tremulously, she hopped off the platform and started toward the changing rooms, but within three steps, he caught her wrist and spun her around. As if shocked, she looked down at his fingers curled around her flesh, then watched him, wide-eyed, as he lifted her hand in his and kissed her knuckles, one by one. "Speaking of dates," he whispered when he was done, "do you have one?"

Surprise and excitement flickered in her gaze, and his smile widened as he watched her struggle for a reply. He should probably ask Cassandra out on a date, start playing up appearances, but the hope he saw in Kate's pretty eyes… He wanted to kiss her eyelids, and track her jaw with his tongue. Then go to the shell of her ear, where he would whisper all sort of things to her, naughty and nice. He wanted to have what his brothers had; he wanted all of that, with Kate.

This talk of marriages of convenience and business mergers…

Did any of it matter to him? If he didn't have Kate?

He didn't deserve her, but he was damned ready to work to get her. He wanted to stop punishing himself, stop blaming himself for people dying, and just dream of all that life and love he felt when he looked at Kate.

"I…" She hesitated, then shook her head, her cheeks coloring pink. "It's best I go on my own."

She quickly pried her hand free and disappeared behind a velvet curtain to change once more.

* * *

Garrett Gage asking her out on a date?

No. Not a date. Garrett Gage asking her out to the wedding.

And he hadn't really asked her. He seemed to be checking whether she already knew whom she'd go with, which was different.

Still. In her heart, her gut, in the way he'd looked at her...*oooh,* how it had felt when he'd asked her that question.

Kate was still reeling at the possibilities as they dropped off Beth and Molly and then rode in silence back to her place. Rain caught up with them by the time he pulled over in front of her one-story house. The drops were so big, they made huge splattering sounds on the windshield and the top of the car.

"Oh, no," Kate groaned.

Garrett reached into the backseat and grabbed his suit jacket. "Remember this? Something like this has saved your pretty head from getting wet before."

The memories surfaced, and when his teeth flashed wide in a white smile, there was no future in Florida, no painful past, only Garrett and his coat, and the rain outside.

He grabbed the door handle. "All right, Kate, here we go."

Heart pounding with emotion as she remembered other times he'd saved her just like this, she watched him sprint around the car and jerk the door open, holding his jacket over both their heads as he pulled her up against his side and onto the sidewalk. As her flats began getting soaked, she pressed close to his massive chest and suddenly his arm slid around her waist, his eyes glinting. “Ready? On three.”

She nodded breathlessly, a gasp already poised in her throat.

“One, two, three!”

They ran for cover to the door, the fresh puddles at their feet splashing at each step as they both burst out laughing. Kate knew this wouldn’t have happened if her catering van hadn’t been parked in the middle of her driveway, but rain in Texas was truly rare and she hadn’t expected it at all.

Once at the door, she struggled to fit the key into the doorknob, and she could hear Garrett breathing at her back as he hunched his shoulders over her, the jacket covering them both.

“Katie, be any slower, and we could just shampoo here already.”

“I’m getting it!” she cried, laughing at her own awkwardness as the angle of the rain managed to get them both wet from the sides. The door clicked open at last, and she hurried inside, turning to see him standing just outside the door, getting wetter by the second. She couldn’t bear to leave him there like that, so she motioned him inside and slammed the door after him. His white shirt clung damply to his back and right side.

She squeezed a couple of raindrops out of the tips of her hair as Garrett shook his jacket in the air and hooked it on the coat stand. When Kate kicked off her shoes, their shoulders touched, and she realized Garrett smelled of fresh rain.

She couldn’t miss the way his broad chest jerked and stretched his white dress shirt with each breath. And she knew her nipples were poking into her dampened blouse;

she caught his dazzlingly sexy white smile as he stared down at her. "Someone looks wet," he said laughingly.

"You should see yourself."

"I'm perfectly aware that I'm wet."

"Take your shirt off, and I'll dry it for you. I'd do the same for your jacket, but I assume it's dry-clean?"

"So is the damn shirt."

"Then at least let me hang it." Without thinking, her hands flew up to start unbuttoning him, and by the time she started to undo the last button, she realized that he'd gone utterly still. His eyes had darkened completely, and emotion clogged Kate's throat as their love-making vividly came back to her mind.

"Katie, if you don't want this—stop me...stop me now...."

He seemed to notice that something had made her hands fall still, for he angled his head downward and peered mischievously into her eyes. "Just say you want me naked and I'll take it all off."

"You're so easy," she scoffed, but she dropped her hands when she realized the danger, and his shirt fell open to reveal his beautiful tan abs. She shouldn't be talking to him. She shouldn't even want to, need to, be close to him. She could have almost kicked herself when she asked, "Do you want some dinner?"

He didn't hesitate, even when the tension between them as palpable.

He followed her through the living room. "I don't want to put you to work."

"It's not work to me. I'll cook us something easy. I hate eating alone and miss Molly terribly," she said.

But was that really why she'd asked him to dinner? Or was it because she knew that as soon as she left San

Antonio, she would never be able to enjoy his company like this again?

"I'm sorry, Kate."

For a moment, she didn't know what he was sorry about. *He's sorry about you missing Molly, Kate. Get your head in the game.* "But she's so happy," she finally answered. She smiled as she eased into the adjoining kitchen, quietly slipping on an apron.

"Aren't you a cute one," Garrett murmured.

His gaze was so openly admiring that Kate's stomach squeezed. She grabbed a knife and gestured dramatically with it. "Flattery will get you equal portions, so don't waste your breath."

"I'm not wasting it. I'm holding it."

Ignoring the butterflies in her stomach, Kate rummaged through the fridge and pulled out her almond flour, eggs, milk and a bunch of vegetables. She set the veggies on a cutting board and transferred them to the kitchen island. "Help me with these while I work on the dough?"

"Of course. Just tell me what to do."

"Cut the mushrooms, red peppers, onions and zucchini into small but pretty slices."

"I can do small, but I don't guarantee pretty." His lips curled upward as he grasped the knife that she offered and his fingers closed warmly over hers.

Shivers of delight shot from the place he touched, and she couldn't suppress the shudder that ran down her limbs. "They're not going to a beauty pageant. Just small will do," she whispered, impulsively pressing in behind him and leaning to watch as she showed him how. She shifted her hands so that he held the knife, and she held *him,* and then she slowly guided him to cut in the size she wanted.

Garrett stood utterly still and compliant, letting her guide him, and suddenly her nipples pressed painfully into his hard back as she realized how intimately her arms were going around his narrow waist.

"What are we making?"

She swallowed when he turned slightly and glanced directly at her. His voice was smooth and calm, but when she spoke, Kate's wasn't. "Vegetable goat-cheese pizza."

He turned back to watch her cut a slice of pepper. "Kate, you're going to kill me."

"Why? I thought you liked it?"

"Exactly. My mouth is watering."

Her cheeks flamed up as she thought of his mouth, and she instantly released him and went back to her spot to prepare the dough. Moments later, she lifted her head when the rhythmical sounds of Garrett's chopping stopped. He was watching her massage the dough. A lock of his dark hair fell over one eye. Her legs weakened at the sexy look, and her heart grew wings in her chest. Garrett looked incredibly beautiful in her kitchen. As beautiful as he did in bed with her.

She opened her mouth to say something, then closed it when her cheeks burned at the memory. She really shouldn't have slept with him. Now she couldn't even look at him without becoming hyperaware of the electricity between them.

A smile slowly formed on his lips as if he could read her thoughts. Then he turned his attention back to his chopping, his profile hard and square, but the expression on his face also thoughtful. Kate swallowed and mixed her dough, then slammed her fists into it and rolled it a couple of more times.

"Bring the veggies once they're cut so you can help me arrange them."

He didn't answer, but soon, he brought over the cutting board. He set it on the counter, and as Kate began to arrange all the little pieces on the flattened pizza crust, his hands gripped her waist from behind. Her breath was knocked out of her when his fingers squeezed her and his lips brushed against her ear.

"Why'd you sleep with me, Kate?" he murmured.

Heat arrowed from her ear straight to her toes, and she stiffened against the dissolving sensation in her bones.

He didn't sound angry. He sounded confused, but patient, much as he did when he wanted to get to the bottom of something.

He surprised her by pressing into her body, trapping her between the counter and himself. Kate had nowhere to go, her spine arching up against his chest as she closed her eyes and tried to still her racing heartbeat.

His voice sounded in her ear as his fingers started a trail up her rib cage. "Did you feel pity for me because I was sick—?"

"No." She could barely utter the word.

"Then why?"

His breath was warm, and damp, and it made her shiver. "It was a mistake. We weren't thinking clearly." Trying to gather her wits, she nervously turned in the cage of his arms, gripped the tray and slid the pizza into the oven, forcing him to step back as she bent forward.

When she shut the door and turned, Garrett had stepped back and merely stood watching her. His snowy-white dress shirt was still parted at the middle, and her saliva glands went crazy at the sight of his bare chest, his flat, hard abs and his belly button.

"Maybe it was a mistake, Kate, one I've spent all my life avoiding. But what if it isn't a mistake?"

Her blood started heating in her veins as she remembered the delicious way he'd moved in her. Kissed her. Gripped her.

She knew they had to talk about this, no matter how much she wished they would pretend nothing had gone on that day. And now that he'd brought up the topic, she could barely think straight. The look in his eyes was beyond intimate. It was downright proprietary, and she almost drowned in the darkness of those eyes that haunted her dreams. With an inhuman effort, she made her way around the kitchen island, putting some distance between them.

His voice stopped her as he followed her around.

"Kate. Answer me. What if it wasn't a mistake?"

Her breath caught in disbelief, and suddenly, she did a one-eighty to face him. "You just want to keep me here, Garrett. You'd do anything to win—that's how you are. And you want to keep me from going to Florida."

"You know me better than that, Freckles."

"I know you're the most stubborn man I know."

He lifted one lone eyebrow. "And you aren't stubborn? You're stubborn *and* proud, Katie. The combo makes for a very difficult lady."

She shook her head but couldn't help smiling. Then she signaled at his damp shirt; it was still driving her crazy how it stuck damply to his beautiful brown nipples. It was about as sexy as him being naked or, strangely, even more so. "Are you taking that shirt off? I can still dry it for you."

He whipped it off, and it gave her something to do as she hooked it on a high kitchen cabinet close to the oven heat. "So that's how you get men naked," he roughly teased.

"Of course. I make it rain, then I strip them." She smoothed her hands down the sleeves to unwrinkle them.

"What do you do after you strip them?"

She stopped fussing over his shirt and realized he was coming closer. His smile was overtly sexual, his dark eyes glimmering in liquid mischief. "Do you kiss them?"

"Maybe," she said and slid past him to go back around the kitchen island. There was something very predatory in his eyes, and she began backing away more quickly as her heart kicked wildly in her rib cage.

"Do you caress them with those hands of yours? Look up at them with those pretty eyes?"

She blinked for a moment, then burst out laughing. "*What* do you mean? These are the only eyes I have. Which others should I use?"

"It's the look in those eyes I refer to. Do you use that doe look on them, too? The one that makes me want to chase you?"

When she laughingly shook her head and backed away farther, he charged and she squealed and sped around the kitchen island, managing two rounds until he caught her and spun her around, both their smiles a mile long. His grin faded before she could even bask in the beauty of it, and his expression fell deathly somber. "I want to kiss you very badly," he whispered, bending his head, his chest heaving.

"Garrett, no," she murmured, struggling to pull free. She spun around and went to check on the pizza, her pulse throbbing in her temples as she pretended to be busy watching the cheese melt.

He came up behind her again and stroked a hand down her hair. "What if I asked you for what you wanted, and you told me exactly what it is that you *want?*"

"Florida."

His stare almost bored holes into her profile, and through the corner of her eye, she noticed his jaw clamped, hard as granite. "Be real with me, Kate. For once in our lives, let's stop playing games."

She shook her head, feeling panicked and afraid of opening up to him. "Whatever it is, you can't give it to me."

"Just try me."

Gnawing on her lower lip, she studied his face, his features carved fiercely in determination, as if he truly did care for her. Well...did he? Had he seen her like a woman all along and had she not noticed because she'd been too busy pretending she didn't love him? She wanted him. All of him. A family of her own. She knew it was too much to want of him, to *ask* from him. Especially after what she'd heard.

"Everyone knows about you and...that heiress you're planning a wedding with."

His eyebrows lifted in mock interest. "Like it's a fact now?"

Ignoring the dangerous purr in his voice, Kate put on an oven mitt, pulled the pizza out and set it on the stove top. "I can't believe you'd marry for business." She couldn't look at him while saying that, so she occupied herself with preparing the food.

He was silent as she used her cutter to slice the pizza into perfect pieces.

Then he murmured, "I wasn't going to marry at all. So why would it matter if I just used it as means to an end, if it's what Cassandra's asking for and it will all be over in six months anyway?"

"You're better than that, Garrett," she whispered.

"But not good enough for you," he mumbled, watching her closely.

Her throat tightened on a reply that she just refused to give as she put a slice on a plate for him, and another on one for herself, staying quiet. What was the point? Flirting with him? Playing with fire? He never wanted to marry, he'd just said, and if he did, it was purely for business. She had to believe she deserved a family of her own. Especially since she'd had her own family torn apart when she was so young.

Quietly, she carried both plates to the kitchen island. He sat down on the stool beside her, then took a large bite, munching.

"Freckles, this is so good." He shook his head and took another bite, making a groaning noise that made her remember…sex. With him.

"It is, isn't it?" The sweet vegetable flavors combined with the toasted-almond flour and goat cheese melted in her mouth, but her insides melted more at the sounds he made. She squirmed on her stool and watched him get up to pour two glasses of water from the pitcher in the fridge.

He set hers down next to her plate, then continued eating. When he licked up a crumb from the corner of his lips, her heart raced in a strange mix of fear and anticipation. He'd asked if she wanted him to give chase… and suddenly she couldn't imagine anything more exhilarating than being hunted, chased and claimed by him.

Shaking her head, she washed down her pizza with the water. She was surprised when he spoke again; he'd already finished his slice. Now his attention seemed fixed solely on her again.

He stroked a finger down her jaw.

"What about me?" he asked.

She frowned and set her half-eaten pizza down. "What do you mean, what about you?"

"You say you'd only marry for love. Do you feel nothing for me? If I go through with this marriage to Cassandra, how would you feel about it?"

The meal suddenly wasn't sitting too well in her stomach. "If she's what you want…"

"I'm very interested in something that she has, but I want to make it clear that I don't want her." There was no mistaking the steel in his voice as he set a hand on her thigh as if it belonged there. "What I want to know is if there's even a chance that I can have what I most want on this earth."

Her pulse skyrocketed when she saw the stark hunger in his gaze, a gaze that ping-ponged from her eyes to her mouth and made her pulse race erratically. But when he began to get close, she stood up for some reason. Garrett laughed darkly, quietly, as if to himself. Then he followed her up and began to back her into a corner with purpose, his eyes blazing.

"Where are you going, Kate?"

She quickened her steps, but he followed closely until she stopped when the back of her knees hit a wall.

He smiled delightedly. "You do want me to catch you, don't you?"

With painstaking slowness, as though to torture her, he raised his hand and set it on her hair, and it was as if she could feel his fingers tangling inside her, tangling around her heart. "Do you want to be with me again?" he rasped, using his fist in her hair to tip her head back.

Every instinct of self-preservation warned her against reaching out to him, giving him this power over her again, but there was no pulling away from him as his hand wound deeper into the fall of hair at her nape, his piercing onyx eyes drowning her in their depths.

"I've been inside you once—and it wasn't enough. I wanted to wake up and look into your eyes and see you smile at me. I didn't want you to leave. Not like that. Not like it was a mistake."

Her breasts rose and fell with each strained breath. "It wasn't a mistake to me. I loved every moment of it."

"Then why don't you put your arms around me now? Why don't you touch me? Was I too rough?" His voice dropped even lower as he tightened his fist, his eyes holding a sexy, primal shine as he drank in her face. "Katie, I promise you that next time I'll take it so much slower. I'll kiss you from the tip of your toes to the top of your lovely head. I'll move slowly inside you…"

He bent his head, tipped up her face with a crooked finger and kissed her parted lips. The gasps stealing out of her were impossible to hold back. He opened his mouth as though to breathe them into his body, drag them into his lungs.

"I'll prepare you for me again. Prepare you for hours, Kate. Hours. I don't regret it happened, Kate, only that I didn't do it right."

He grasped her hands and placed them on his shoulders, and Kate didn't take them away. Her nails gouged into his skin as she pressed against him, her eyes drifting shut. "Please don't do this."

"How long will you hold out, Kate? If I do this..."

Expert fingers traced the tips of her sensitive breasts through her damp shirt, and Kate gasped as sensations stormed through her.

"Will you say no? If I do this...?"

He undid her halter top and let the fabric pool at her waist, and then eased one breast out of the material of her bra. He bent his head and kissed one straining nipple, laving it expertly with his tongue, priming it before he latched on and suckled her with his warm mouth.

Moisture pooled between her legs, red-hot desire rocking to her very core.

She clasped his head, thinking to pull him back, but instead she just clutched his silky hair as he turned his head and performed the same expert torture on the other puckered tip.

She struggled weakly, halfheartedly, until he pressed her arms down at her sides, their fingers linking in a tight grip as he took her mouth in a wild, stormy kiss. Her lips opened, allowing him entrance with a soft, welcoming moan, and she was undone by his taste. "Garrett."

Not even thinking what she was doing, Kate clung to him and curled one leg around his hips, her skirt hiking up as she nestled his hardness between her open thighs.

He curled a hand around the back of her knee to keep her leg up, and he rocked his hips and pulled back to stare into her wide, sparkling eyes. He bent down to take her lips softly. "You want that, Katie? You want that from me?"

The feel of him, the reminder of what it felt like to have him, hot and hard, inside her, made her feverish.

She wanted to nod, to say yes, to tell him not to ask

and just take her, but instead she wedged a hand between their burning bodies and palmed his erection. He hissed out a breath and nipped her earlobe, the closest thing to his mouth, then swept down to devour one aching nipple again.

She moaned feebly and began to pant. Arching her back, she pushed her breast up, as if craving a deeper kiss, so he opened wide around her flesh and sucked hard. "Garrett!" she cried.

A groan rumbled up in his chest as he seized her hands and pinned them over her head, trapping her as he looked at her with wild, hungry eyes.

"I want this so much." He ducked his head and his lips brushed the tip of her breast, his hand tightening on her wrists.

She felt a new surge of dampness in her panties, her breasts weighing heavily with the need to be cupped by his palms. Kate couldn't believe how many times she'd dreamed of this, wanted it. She moaned softly and arched her back in invitation once more.

"Garrett..." She pressed herself up to his mouth, and his lips returned to her nipple. Fire swept through her.

Fisting her flowing, flaming hair in his hands, he pulled her face back to look at him. "Tell me you want me." He spoke in a dangerous tone as his hands slid downward to unzip her skirt.

"I want you," she gasped.

He kissed her hard, blindingly, as he shoved the material down her hips, then slid her clinging halter top off, as well.

His lips softened on a groan as he cupped her sex in his big palm. His voice was but a breath in her ear, shaking her world like a cannon blast. "I want you, too. I can't stop wanting you."

He pressed the heel of his palm to the bundle of nerves hidden at her core, and she released a soft cry.

He dipped his hand into her panties, then watched her as he parted her folds with his fingers and pushed the middle one inside. Her hips rolled while her eyes searched his face and he pushed her arousal even higher.

"Does one feel good? Or would you rather have two?" he rasped.

He watched her expression dissolve as he added a second finger into her snug grip. A surge of moisture drenched his hand, and he bent his head and prodded a taut nipple with his tongue.

That's when he heard voices out in the living room.

Kate snapped out of her daze and stiffened when she heard the front door slam shut. She practically flew away from Garrett, jumping as the voices became clear and the two figures appeared in the living room—which adjoined the kitchen.

"—so just be quiet and let me get it real qui…"

Molly and Julian froze in their tracks.

Molly's eyes flared in mute shock as Kate struggled to right her bra and panties and used the vegetable chopping block to cover what she could. Julian's eyes widened like saucers as he took in Garrett's bare-chested state and Kate trying her damnedest to hide behind one miserable little cutting board.

"Okay, I'd rather not have seen that. What about you, Molls?" Julian smirked.

Molly blinked, her cheeks about as red as her hair, but Kate was sure she wasn't nearly as red as Kate. "Seen what? I didn't see anything. I think I'll come visit with Kate another day."

They shuffled backward through the living room, and even after the front door slammed shut behind them, Kate just couldn't look at Garrett. Her face burned in embarrassment. They were panting, the sounds of their haggard breaths echoing in the silence. Slowly, he reached out, but she stepped back and shook her head.

"What is it you want from me, Garrett?" she asked brokenly.

His voice was low and textured with wanting. "I want you to stay in the city, Kate."

"Is that all?"

"For now, yes." His face tightened with emotion as he watched her slip back into her skirt, and his eyes flashed as he saw her reach for her discarded clothing. "Fine, no."

"Then what?" Her arms shook as she shoved them back into the arm holes.

"I want you in bed with me." His eyes raked down her body almost desperately, and she hated how easily her blood bubbled again when he grabbed her hands to stop her from dressing. "Please. Kate. Don't."

"So this is about sex," she said. She pushed his hands away.

"You make it sound like that's a bad thing. Katie, I know you want me, too. You were just trembling in my arms."

"For how long do you want me in bed? A week? Two?" she dared, her heart twisting in her chest when she tried to recall if Garrett had ever really even been with anyone for that long. "What about Cassandra? Don't you think she'd like to know about your little side plan here?"

His mouth dipped into an even deeper scowl than usual, then he restlessly raked his fingers through his hair. "Damn, Katie, I keep feeling like I'm falling short here. What the hell is it that you *want* from me?"

"You're talking about marriage with another woman, Garrett! And you stand here telling me you fall short? You damned well do fall short! If I'd wanted an affair, I'd have it with someone other than you. I want a shot at having the family I've never had, that's what I want!"

In the instant she spoke those last words, Kate wished she could take them back. It was as though she'd slapped him; Garrett suddenly looked like that young boy, that dark, tormented young boy, so forlorn after what had happened the night of the murders.

"Well, then you were right about one thing," he said, a tinge of angry frustration in his voice. "I can definitely not give you back what you want."

"Garrett, you misunderstood me—"

But he was gone, the bang of the door that followed his departure making her wince.

Eight

Garrett knew that their half brother, Emerson Wells, harbored no love for the Gages. Even though the Gage patriarch had apparently been screwing Emerson's mother for years, he'd refused to recognize Emerson as his son and bought the woman off to stay quiet and away from them—something the family had discovered when their father's lawyer, upon his death, disclosed the existence of another heir who could contest part of the inheritance.

He never did, though Eleanor Gage had thought it wise to pay him a few million dollars to go away for good.

Naturally, if Emerson had half the clout and pride of a Gage—which he apparently did—he would have no intention of ever catering to a Gage's wishes. So he'd denied Landon's summons six times during the past several weeks, something that didn't surprise Garrett. But now, they were running out of time to make concrete decisions about the Clarks Communications deal, and Garrett finally had it with begging the imbecile for a meeting. This limbo was putting everyone on edge, especially him, since not only his two brothers, but Cassandra herself, seemed to believe Garrett was the only one who could make the deal possible now.

He'd been so close to just saying, "To hell with it, I'll do it."

Kate would never have him anyway.

And yet a little part of him knew that he could never stop trying. Not now. Not when he knew that she wanted him, knew the delicate feel of her body against his, knew the fragrance of that devilishly sexy red hair. Kate might not know it yet, and hell, Garrett might have spent his entire life fighting it, but they belonged to one another.

The recent times they'd seen one another at his mother's Sunday brunches, they'd spoken of trivial things, their last argument forgotten—or at least, not mentioned. But the air crackled between them. Her eyes seemed bluer when they rested on him. They softened when she saw him. He wasn't blind to it, couldn't be blind to those looks anymore. He had to do something, and fast.

So that's how he'd found himself sitting in his office yesterday, dialing Emerson's mother. He was surprised that she'd picked up after a few rings.

"This is Garrett Gage, and I realize Emerson doesn't want to hear from us, but it's imperative we talk to him. I assure you he'll be happy to hear us out, if you could—"

The woman had hung up.

But Garrett hadn't given up. He'd then punched in some numbers and got Emerson's secretary on the line.

After a moment of silence, she'd put him on hold. When she finally came back, she'd reluctantly conceded, "He'll give you ten minutes tomorrow morning."

Now, as he presented himself at his half brother's office downtown, he marveled at how well his brother seemed to be doing for himself. Garrett strolled through the floor containing the executive offices and found his brother's secretary waiting for him. "Mr. Wells will be here shortly, Mr. Gage. You can go right in."

He grabbed a mint from the plate on her desk as she continued typing on her keyboard, and instead of taking a seat, he paced around while the woman continued typing. After taking a phone call, she hung up and left her desk, and Garrett knew exactly where he would wait for his brother. He strolled directly into the sumptuous office with the plaque EMERSON WELLS, PRESIDENT on the door. He took the seat in front of Emerson's desk and laced his fingers behind his head as he waited, taking in his surroundings with an admiring eye. Apparently his half brother appreciated art—he had a vitrine full of pre-Columbian artifacts that stretched across an entire wall. There were no photographs on his desk; in fact, there were hardly any personal effects at all.

After a few more minutes the man arrived, and his murderous expression told Garrett he didn't like seeing him one bit.

But he *had* agreed to the appointment, at last.

Emerson sighed and crossed his arms. "Which one of the three brothers are you?"

"The middle one," Garrett said.

Emerson's expression softened somewhat at the news, and for a moment, Garrett even sensed that he'd dropped his guard a little. His voice was still wary, though. "So you're the one who was there when Father died."

Garrett's insides went icy cold at the reminder, but he still managed a curt nod, though Emerson hadn't seemed to phrase it as a question anyway.

"He say anything about me?" Emerson asked, and Garrett flashed back to the sidewalk, the street, the concert they'd just come from that night.

Chest knotting up painfully, Garrett dragged in a long, steadying breath. "He tried to speak, but he couldn't get much out."

The talk about his father made the memory so goddamned fresh now, his stomach roiled. He thought back to Dave Devaney's last breath, and to Kate. The way her face had crumpled when the police had brought Garrett home and he'd told everyone that both men were dead.

Kate wanted a family. A family she'd never had, because of *him*.

There hadn't been a night since she'd said that when he hadn't recalled her words. He hadn't been able to face her a moment longer. She'd torn him open and apart, and for weeks he'd been grappling for ways in which he could ever make it up to her. Would he never be able to put it behind him? Was she leaving because Garrett reminded her too much of what she couldn't have? Or because she'd never forgive him for repeatedly screwing up her life?

Shaking the disturbing thought aside, he stood up and stuck his hands into his pants pockets, assuming a casual stance as they faced each other. "I can tell you want me gone, so I'll happily drop the chitchat. My brothers and I want to make a deal with you. We're not interested in making friends, and we know you aren't either. What we're interested in is business, and judging by the luxurious surroundings and the Picasso on the wall, you're a man who thinks of business just as we do. Am I right?"

Though he was dark-haired like Garrett, Emerson's eyes weren't the same. He had Landon's silver eyes instead, and they glowed eerily with warning. "My father ran me over like a goddamned mongrel without a tail. I won't allow the same from you."

"I'm sorry that he felt he had to," Garrett said, but he understood what his father was trying to protect. He hadn't wanted his wife to ever find out he'd strayed. So he'd cut off his illegitimate son and lover from his life, only to die so soon afterward that his lawyers had still been paying off the woman for her silence when it happened.

It had been tragic, to watch his mother find out she'd been betrayed. When she could do nothing about it.

She'd been broken at the funeral—crying nonstop at first, already having found out from the accounts, and the lawyers, her husband had not been the faithful, loving man she'd always imagined. Garrett had had his own grief on his shoulders, and he'd blamed himself for the pain he saw on her mother's face. His mother would have never found out about Emerson, or another woman, if her husband hadn't died so abruptly and she hadn't been forced to take over the financials of the family. The records of money sent to another woman's account, regularly, sparked alarm, confusion, until finally, the truth had sunk in.

"He freaking ruined my life. He broke my mother's heart and mine, too," Emerson grated, his teeth tightly clamped as he curled his fingers into fists.

Garrett was taken aback by the hard anger in his half

brother's eyes. Would Cassandra Clarks be able to handle being married to this guy for six months? He appeared only half-civilized, and dangerous, to boot.

"Emerson, I'm sorry if the measures he took were not to your liking, but your mother liked them very well," Garrett said. He was referring to the three million-dollar payments she'd received for her silence—after his father died. Not to mention that he'd already been providing for her to have quite a healthy living while he was still alive. Emerson couldn't have been more than twelve at the time. Julian had barely been ten. Garrett had been fifteen and Landon eighteen.

If their father hadn't died, Emerson would be walking the streets without the Gage brothers ever knowing he existed.

Maybe they should have tried to contact him. Maybe Emerson resented that, too. But just seeing the grief on their mother's face had been enough to make them want to keep him as far away from the family as they could.

Maybe, all hell would break loose when Mother once again realized they were dealing with him. But Landon had said that he'd take care of Mother. Enough time had passed that hopefully she'd look beyond her dead husband's transgressions at this point. And their mother was shrewd when it came to business, too.

"Will you meet with me and my brothers to discuss our business proposition? We really need your help."

Impatient, Garrett waited for Emerson's answer, but his half brother only glared at him as he slowly headed over to resume his place behind his desk.

Emerson was more rugged than all his brothers, and even with his well-groomed appearance in that gray suit, there was an air of isolation around his tall figure that made Garrett somehow relate to him. He knew that Emerson was somewhere between Julian and Garrett in age, so that put him around twenty-eight or twenty-nine. His hair was dark as Garrett's, his face as square and tan, but personality-wise, he seemed to be a wild card.

"I'll give you a half hour," Emerson finally conceded, his expression unreadable as he dropped into his chair and powered on his computer. "But not today. I have too much to do."

"Fine," he agreed. "Tomorrow then. Be at the *Daily* at nine a.m."

"No can do. I'm afraid I can only do it Friday."

Friday wasn't ideal. It was three days from now and only a day before the wedding. But Garrett ground his molars, shut the hell up and took the offer. Something in Emerson's angry expression when he looked up and gestured at the door to signal the conservation was over told Garrett this offer was the best he'd get from him.

"Don't be late," Garrett growled as he left.

"Kate, I'm calling and calling and no answer, then I come to get the things for the shower and they're not even baked! What is wrong with you? It's ten in the morning and we have work to do. This is our last gig before we're swept away with all this wedding stuff. You didn't talk to anyone all weekend. What's the matter? It's Tuesday. A new day awaits!"

Kate groaned when a chirpy Beth yanked open her bedroom curtains and a shaft of sunlight sliced between Kate's eyelids. She waved a weak hand in the air and rolled onto her stomach.

"Go away, Beth."

"No, I'm not going away. You, my sleepy little chef, will stand up, take a shower and—"

"I'm pregnant," Kate groaned.

"—get to work. What did you just say?"

Kate covered her face with the pillow and screamed into its feathery depths while kicking off the sheets tangled around her ankles. "I'm pregnant. *God!* I'm such a fool. Fool, fool, *fool*."

"You're pregnant as in…you're with *child?*"

Kate sat up and cracked open her puffy eyes. "Three tests, Beth. Three. And they all agree on the fact that I'm preggo. What am I going to do?"

Sighing in misery, she covered her face with her hands, refusing to answer the string of startled, quick-fire questions Beth bombarded her with next. *"Well, whose is it? When did this happen? Why didn't you tell me? When did you find out, damn it? Are you sure?"*

Oh, Beth. She was like a bright little shooting star today—a bright little shooting star in Kate's dark gray world.

Was Kate sure? Yes, she was sure. The test stick couldn't get any pinker! The two lines, almost neon in their brightness, had been clear enough to spin Kate into a whirlwind of despair all through the night.

While miserably pondering what to do, Kate heard Beth shuffle around the room, no doubt in search of the pregnancy tests. Beth was big on evidence and that sort of thing. This came from being married to a douche bag before she'd fallen in love with Landon.

When her friend couldn't seem to find them, Kate muttered, "They're in the trash, Beth."

"Oh."

Beth disappeared into the bathroom. Kate glumly

wondered what Garrett would do when he eventually found out she was carrying his baby. She remembered how handsome he'd looked two Sundays ago at brunch. He had been thoughtful and dark as sin, and staring at her so intently and so intimately, Kate had barely been able to eat anything. She'd felt eaten by *him*. He'd stood to follow her when she'd gone to pretend to fill her plate at the buffet, and she'd felt his hand at the small of her back. "You all right?" he'd murmured.

"Of course. Why wouldn't I be?"

"You've been so busy with work, I keep wondering if you're avoiding me."

"I'm sorry. We can talk at the rehearsal dinner…that is, if you don't…if you're not bringing…"

"I won't bring anyone if you won't," he said, staring at her intently.

"I won't," she assured him.

"Then I won't," he said back.

And oh, how she wished she had the courage to say she was sorry for what she'd said to him that day in her apartment, but the continued talk she heard from Molly and Beth regarding the Clarks and Gage wedding was driving her insane with jealousy and anger.

It killed her. How could he? How dare he tell her he wanted her in his bed while he was planning his brilliant and very convenient wedding? The desire that had whipped them up like tornadoes had now dropped them hard on land, and the whirlwind and the emotions in the air had been reduced to nothing.

Nothing but a one-night stand, that's what it had been.

But of course, good ol' Murphy's law had come for a visit and made *sure* Kate got pregnant.

And now they were going to have a child together.

"Yes. You're pregnant," Beth agreed when she came back out of the bathroom.

A silence settled bleakly in the room.

You're pregnant....

Her chest gripped with yearning. Along with the inexplicable fear of dying alone, without a family or anyone to love her, Kate had harbored another kind of fear for years. It was one of those little fears that took root in you and you never really knew why you had them—only that you did.

She'd feared she'd prove infertile when she grew up, and that she'd never be able to have the family she'd always longed for. She'd imagined, on her best days, that if she ever got pregnant, the thrill she'd feel would obliterate anything else.

Now, maybe a little kernel of thrill had taken up residence somewhere, in some quiet, motherly part of her, but it was too hidden to recognize.

Kate had proven fertile, yes. Physically capable of having a family, yes.

But she had conceived this baby with Garrett Gage.

And her considerable pride already smarted like *hell* since she knew she would have to tell him. Especially after this past month, when they'd both pretended at the family Sunday brunches that they were still just friends.

Kate saw that Beth had her cell phone in her hand and leaped out of bed. "No! What are you doing?"

Beth held the phone out of Kate's reach, her expression stern as a concerned mother's. "I'm calling a doctor. Unless you want me to call Garrett, Kate. It's his, isn't it? You look pale, Kate. I think—"

"Call anyone and die. Do you hear me?"

The thought of Garrett knowing this so soon, before

she had time to build up her emotional walls against him…the thought of him finding out that just the thought of carrying his baby inside her made her queasy and restless…and the thought of him demanding to *marry* her out of duty and honor and all he held dearer than Kate…

No. God, it was worse than she could imagine.

Her worst nightmare come true.

Beth paused when she noticed the angry flush spreading up Kate's neck. Lips pursed, she hung up, and started dialing again.

"No! Beth, don't you *dare*."

"I'm calling Molly, okay? We need to figure out how we're handling this with the family. Don't even try to stop me this time."

Kate groaned. "Molly's getting her paintings shipped to New York, and she's got enough on her plate with a wedding in five days!"

"Fine, then Julian. Julian will help us with this, Kate, you know he will."

An image of hunky, easygoing Julian, never judgmental, always one for cool-headed thoughts, flitted through her mind. Julian had always been the perfect coconspirator. Not only did he know how to stay quiet, it was his nature to.

But Kate still shook her head. "Beth, the wedding is in five days. Let's just…drop this for now. Please. Please don't tell anyone until I'm ready."

Beth met her eyes dubiously. "But what are you going to do when you see Garrett at the rehearsal dinner? At the wedding? When are you going to tell him?"

"After the wedding. I can't do it before. I want Molly to enjoy her day," she said miserably.

"No, no, no, that's not a good plan. It might be too

late, Kate. He might be engaged by then to another woman!"

Pain wrenched through Kate's insides. "I don't expect him to stop his plans for me. Honestly. We could be better parents if we weren't together than if we are forced to be together."

"You're afraid, Kate, and that's okay. But you're turning into a coward. Where's the girl I know? The Kate I know would fight for him. Stop being afraid that he will break your heart. You're breaking it yourself without even letting him know that he has it."

Kate couldn't reply.

But the words replayed in her head like an echo of a truth she wasn't sure she was prepared to listen to when she had a pregnancy to deal with.

Was Beth right?

Was Kate so afraid of letting him in that she was running away, not from being hurt by him, but from *loving* him?

Oh, God. And now what was she going to do about Miami?

Nine

Kate was turning out to be one of those pregnant women who had nausea every morning, and it wasn't fun at all. But at least by Thursday evening at Molly and Julian's rehearsal dinner at the Gage mansion, she felt better. The wedding was to be held this upcoming Saturday at noon, and the gardens had been bursting with activity all day as contractors had started delivering tables, chairs…the works. Through the windows on the other side of the living room, Kate could see the beautiful white trellis that would serve as the chapel, halfway to being fully erected.

It was going to be a beautiful wedding.

Her heart soared as she watched Molly and Julian laugh while talking to the minister. Julian towered behind Molly, who seemed to be leaning back against him as if he were a pillar. His arms were loosely around her, his chin resting on the top of her head.

There was no doubt in Kate's mind when she saw them that they belonged together. Molly had always loved Julian, but Kate hadn't realized that Julian had loved her sister back until a couple of months ago.

She'd always believed in having one soul mate…until, at eighteen, she'd realized that the man she thought might be her soul mate didn't seem to agree. He'd never openly touched her like Julian had touched Molly, but now she kept remembering the way he'd made love to her.

Did he *care* about her? Or was this all about her leaving?

"There you are!" Kate heard the booming voice of Eleanor Gage from nearby, and in the same instant, spotted the person she was speaking to as he came into the room.

Dressed in a black suit and gleaming silver tie, Garrett made such a striking figure that the atmosphere altered dramatically with him near. His beautiful face looked thoughtful and intense as he kissed his mother on the cheek, then lifted his head and seemed to be scanning the area for something. His gaze stopped roaming when he saw her, and she couldn't breathe.

With an expression almost of relief, he came over. He had such purpose in his step, and her heart almost stopped when she saw the way his eyes glimmered with…happiness?

Oh, God, she was going to die when she had to tell him.

"We should've driven over together."

His liquid black eyes raked her figure, and her pulse skyrocketed as though he could suddenly see with some sort of X-ray vision the little baby growing inside her.

For a moment she thought he knew. He knew her secret and it would all be out in the open.

Drawing in a deep breath, she blew a loose strand of hair out of her face. "I hitched a ride with Beth and Landon." The thought of being alone with him in the close confinement of his car again both terrified and excited her.

The more distance she kept from him, the smoother her plans would run.

He seized her elbow and pulled her along the room, leading her to the terrace doors. "Come with me outside."

"Why?"

"Because I want to talk to you, Kate."

She let him lead her to the exact spot they'd visited on his birthday, when he'd found out she was leaving. Rather than release her, his hand stayed on her elbow as he smiled and took in her dress with the thirsty eyes of a man who intimately knew her.

The situation worsened when he bent his head and his voice caressed her ear, its texture a seductive black velvet. "So what have you been up to? Besides avoiding me?"

She ducked, not wanting him to know he still made her knees weak, her insides mushy. She wished—goodness, she wished—that Garrett wasn't considering marriage to another woman, so that Kate wouldn't dread the moment she'd have to mention a child was on the way so much.

"Working and…packing."

"Packing," he repeated without any inflection whatsoever.

The fact that his hand was on her elbow, causing all sorts of ripples of want inside her, made her drop her gaze to take in the contrast of his tan skin with her fair complexion. As though that were an instruction for him to let go, he dropped his hold.

His eyebrows pulled low over his eyes—eyes that were hard with frustration.

"Kate, honestly, what the hell are you running from?"

Anger flared inside her. What else would she be running away from but him? "What do you care if I leave? Why are you so hell-bent on stopping me? Go and worry about your heiress!"

"I will, but you come first, Kate. You've always come first for me. Before anything in the world. And I happen to be responsible for you, Kate."

"Oh puhleeze! Responsible, my fanny. I'm a grown woman, Garrett, a fact that you can attest to yourself. Why do insist on continuing to treat me like your sister?"

"Sister? Kate, I freaking *slept with you!*"

Her eyes widened in shock. Her throat clogged with emotion, and she spun around toward the glass doors. "I can't do this right now. Not here. Not now."

He stopped her with one hand. "I'm sorry, I didn't mean to upset you. But it would be very damn simple for me to marry an heiress right now if it weren't for the fact that you and I made love, Kate."

"We had se—"

"We made love."

His eyes glowed down at her fiercely. Crazily, she even thought she saw longing there. But if he longed for her, why would he even consider marrying anyone else?

"I told you it was a mistake. Please just carry on with your plans, and I'll carry on with mine."

"God, you're so stubborn, Kate." He propped his elbows next to hers on the balustrade and gazed outside, his expression pained. "You'll never be able to forget your father died because of me, will you?"

She swallowed and shook her head. "No. That's not true. I don't blame you, Garrett. You were just a boy, and you wanted to help your father. Like you always want to help everyone. You misunderstood what I said. I might have blamed you for a time because I needed someone to blame. I was so angry."

"Me, too." He leaned forward and stared at the cluttered tables and chairs out on the lawn, and Kate watched his profile as the urge to touch him began to consume her.

"But my anger isn't about that now. It's about me. It angers me to want something that I can't have."

He glanced at her curiously, his head cocked to the side as he patiently waited for her to explain.

"Having a family is something I've wanted my whole life," she admitted, softly.

He dragged her into his arms, and she was so exhausted from learning she was pregnant, she closed her eyes and let him. His thumb stroked her arm, causing goose bumps to jump along her bare flesh.

"I never thought I'd have one of my own, and now I can't stop thinking about it," he whispered.

Fighting to ignore the sensual stirring inside her, Kate closed her eyes, her connection with him too great to ignore. She suddenly wanted to cry, right here in his arms, at his confession. Because she was sure he was imagining having a family with someone else, with a woman he might marry for convenience. Not with Kate. Still, she loved him so much she couldn't hate him for wanting the same thing that she did.

"You deserve to be happy, Garrett. You've tried to take care of all of us for so long. Even Julian and Molly."

He rubbed her back and she rubbed his. "They hate me for making them keep their hands to themselves until now." His whisper stirred the top of her hair.

His scent made her light-headed but instead of drawing away, she drew closer and inhaled, happy that he had an arm around her. "You've always tried to do the right thing."

His lips twitched against her scalp, and he edged back and glanced down at her, searching her expression. "You've always trusted me, Katie. To do the right thing. But you don't trust I'll make the right choice with Cassandra?"

Her stomach twisted uncomfortably, and when she attempted to pry free, Garrett kept her pinned to him. Even his eyes held her trapped. "Relax. Let's not fight, all right? Let me just hold you like this."

His body emanated heat, and her every cell perfectly recalled the night she had belonged to him. Kate's throat closed so tight she couldn't talk, especially when she settled down against him once more. He ran a hand tenderly down the back of her head, and she relaxed her muscles despite herself.

"Katie, let me make it better for you," he whispered against the top of her head.

Kate closed her eyes. She knew he felt compelled to watch over her, but Garrett had been tied to his promise and had looked at her as a *duty* his whole life.

Kate would rue the day she ever trapped him any further.

But now she was carrying his baby.

"If you leave—" he tipped her chin back to look at

her "—who's to tell me it isn't your way of making me come get you?"

She edged back, wide-eyed, then scowled. "I would never do that! I don't want you to…do anything. Plus, it would be hard for you to follow me with a new wife attached to your arm."

"A wife I will not have if I choose not to," he said. "Why don't you tell me why you're so interested in her if you're not interested in staying here?"

She glared, and suddenly it was just too painful to look at him.

She shook her head, and turned to walk away but he wasn't letting her go just yet.

"Where are you going, Katie?" he taunted. "Do I frighten you? Is it me you're running away from?"

She was struggling, but he caught her and looked fiercely into her eyes. His breath fanned her face, slow and steady, warm and unexpectedly sweet.

"Garrett…" she whispered, dying with want as she clutched his shoulders.

He squeezed her. "Kate, I've known you all my life. I've been there for you all my life—I have to be there for the rest of it. You have to let me. We need to talk about what happened. We can't just pretend that it didn't when I'm consumed with knowing that it *did*."

Her eyes were fastened to his mouth, and all she could think of was that his mouth was *there* for her. His lips were there to sear her again, brand her again. Kate trembled with the need to wrap herself around his shoulders and neck and never let go. She wanted to crush his mouth with hers and do all the things she hadn't done with anyone else because she'd been waiting for the boy she secretly loved to *look* at her.

Now he was looking at her. His gaze hungry, missing no detail of her features. Almost seeing into her soul, discovering her secret, aching love for him.

"Tell me why you're leaving. Is it because of me?" He couldn't seem to help himself as he lifted his finger to trace her lips. Her breath caught, and his face darkened as he watched.

Kiss him. Tell him it's him and that he's going to be a father! But while all these impulses rampaged through her, she drew back an inch and considered it a good moment to retreat before she truly lost her senses. She'd lost them once. Now she was pregnant. She didn't want to castigate him for that night, a night she had been wishing and praying would someday happen. She didn't want him to pay with his whole life. She simply loved him too much.

Kate shook her head and glanced away. "No, it's not you."

Spinning away before she could lose her head, she hugged herself and stared into the house, where there was light and music and smiles everywhere.

"You could be carrying my—" Garrett cleared his throat behind her "—you could be pregnant, Kate."

The air felt static as she turned back to him in alarm. "Excuse me?"

The intensity in his eyes terrified her. "We didn't use protection, Freckles."

She shook her head. Fast. Almost too fast.

"You'd tell me if there were consequences, right?" he asked meaningfully.

Her world tilted on its axis. What if she went ahead and told him that she was having his child? Her stomach cramped at the thought.

She was loath to worry Molly a day before her wedding. Kate was the eldest and had cared for her like a mother, had always set a good example. How could she bear detracting from her sister's joy right now?

She had to wait until after the wedding.

She bit her lip, glancing away. "Whatever happens, I meant what I said. I'm not marrying ever without love."

"Why? Do you love another man?"

Swallowing, Kate met his stormy black gaze. "No, Garrett. It would have been hard for me to love anyone, when my whole life I've been in love with you."

He blinked at her words.

God.

She couldn't believe she'd said them.

But she had.

She had to come clean.

She glanced away, blushing. "That's why I slept with you that night, Garrett. And that's why I'm leaving. I want to be loved back."

He stared at her as though flabbergasted, motionless and unmoving.

"We need to go. Dinner is about to be served," she murmured and went inside.

He didn't follow her for minutes, and from inside, she saw him leaning on the balustrade with his face in his hands, breathing hard.

Her insides knotted with pain for him. Maybe she shouldn't have confessed it. But Beth was right. Kate was a coward, afraid he'd hurt her. She'd had to at least let him know that all the time they'd spent together had meant everything to Kate, even when she knew he had not ever been emotionally available to love her like she wanted him to.

Garrett was a fair man. He was a man who recognized his own flaws, maybe even to the extreme extent that he saw flaws where none existed. She knew he felt…unworthy. That he believed a man had died because of him. But he was also generous and giving, and he wouldn't be able to stand the idea of causing Kate any pain.

He'd let her go so she could find what she was looking for, especially once he recognized that he wouldn't be able to give it to her himself. And he'd marry his heiress, for whom he wouldn't need to feel anything. But at least Kate had stopped lying to him and to herself about not loving him anymore. At least she'd told him her real reasons for leaving.

Baby or not, she would still go.

Once they were seated at the tables in the formal dining room, she felt him stare at her as intently as ever from across the floral centerpiece.

Waiters brought over the salads first—arugula, organic pear, goat cheese and candied pecans, topped with a soft vinaigrette dressing with a hint of pomegranate. That was followed by an assortment of lamb, duck, beef tenderloins and chicken medallions, accompanied by the most deliciously spiced vegetables Kate had ever tasted.

She ate whatever she was served and almost still felt a little hungry. But most of all, she was conscious of everything Garrett did on the opposite side of the table. Under the table, she held her hands over her stomach, where she could feel and sense her baby, feeling almost nostalgic that the father was so close, and didn't even know what he'd just given her.

She stole peeks at him throughout the night as idle conversation abounded. When their eyes met, emotions and confusion flooded her.

Once they were enjoying a variety of sorbet, cheese, and sweet desserts, Landon pushed his chair back and stood. "Cheers! To Julian and Molly," Landon said, and glanced at Garrett.

Kate saw the manner in which Garrett nodded somberly at Landon, almost as though saying, "You're next," and Kate jerked her eyes down at her plate, the nausea suddenly coming back with a vengeance.

But no matter how fervently she wished it, there was no taking back her *I love you.*

The next morning, all three Gage brothers sat across the conference table from their half brother. Garrett noticed how Landon and Julian were taking stock of their brother. Emerson was beastly in size, very large and muscled. As president of his personal security business, it seemed fitting, but today Emerson was also proving to be a very moody man. He'd seemed impatient to leave from the moment he arrived.

It seemed truly unjust to Garrett that his father had treated Emerson and his mother the way he had. And when he'd died, he'd ended up hurting everyone, for the truth easily had come to light. Their lawyers had had to explain to the Gages, once they took over all the financial accounts, why there were so many transfers and payments made to an unknown woman.

When they'd learned it was because this woman had borne a Gage son, Garrett's mother had entered a wild depression for years, and he didn't even want to think of how it had been for Emerson and his mother. It had hurt the Gages to lose their father to death, but the pain of losing him while he was living might possibly be even worse.

Now every bit of pain and resentment marked Emerson's hard, unyielding features. Garrett couldn't know the true extent of his resentments, but he'd bet they ran deeper than the man let on. His energy was too controlled, and his eyes were too ruthless and sharp to reveal his emotions.

Garrett knew it would hardly matter to Cassandra which man she married as long as she got out of her brother's clutches, and he and his brothers would be happy to compensate Emerson for the task.

If, that was, they could convince the stubborn man to agree to this whole scenario.

With a bleak, tight-lipped smile, Emerson finally spoke after Landon explained the situation. "If this chick is as hot as you all say, why don't *you* marry her?" he asked, silver eyes trained on Garrett.

"Garrett's not inclined to marry," Landon answered. He sat calmly in his leather chair on the opposite side of the conference table.

"Well, that makes two of us," Emerson said with a growl. "I'm never marrying, especially no damn heiress."

"You might like to reconsider with what we're offering," Landon said, signaling at the open folder sitting before him on the table. "You'll be a very rich man, Emerson, if you agree to this."

"I'm already very rich without needing to deal with any of you."

"Emerson, we're talking fifty million for your take *alone*. That's almost ten million a month for just marrying her."

"Why don't *you* do it?" he persisted, glaring at Garrett.

Garrett wasn't going to tell him why.

But he still remembered Kate in his arms on the terrace last night. He'd been so damned excited to have her in his arms. He'd wanted to make love to her again, had been more than ready to physically. He could have moved back so that she wouldn't notice, and perhaps she hadn't, but instead he'd remained in place, his every sense attuned to her, to the contact of their bodies—the press of her belly against his erection. He'd wanted to press harder into her, to devour her and break her every resistance until she gave him everything he wanted, and admitted to everything he needed to know. At the same time, he wanted to protect her from everything and everyone.

He hadn't pushed, but he knew the thought of leaving was killing her. He knew Molly's wedding had to get to her. Kate was a woman. And she was the older sister, almost like a mother to Molly.

He wanted her. Needed her with a force he'd never needed anyone in his life. Physically, he wanted to be with her again, but it was more. It had always been more with her. *She loved him....*

But he wasn't going to tear his guts open in front of Emerson, not even in front of his other brothers, so when silence reigned, Emerson sighed and rose.

"Sit down, Emerson. I'm planning to marry someone else," Garrett snapped, scowling because he'd had to let the cat out of the bag.

Emerson plopped back down and cocked a brow. "Should I start renting a tux?" he asked, his cockiness reminding Garrett of his younger brother, Julian, somehow.

"Rent it for your own wedding. You won't be coming to mine."

"*My* own wedding is tomorrow and we need this engagement settled. So are you in, or are you out, Emerson?" Julian demanded.

Emerson eyed Julian, then Landon, then Garrett, then Landon again. "There's only one thing that would ever tempt me to agree to this farce."

"Name it and it's yours," said Landon with his business voice.

"I want the Gage name. I'm as much his son as you are. My mother provided a paternity test, and he refused to acknowledge me. I want it acknowledged today. If I get my rightful name, you have a deal."

Garrett crossed his arms and eyed Landon, who seemed to be the one most reluctant to grant Emerson's wish. Garrett wasn't against it. The Gage brothers had no right to withhold something their own father should have granted his kid in the first place, but they would need to talk to their mother first. She was a just woman, but she might need some time to get used to the idea of a fourth Gage in town.

In a terse but quiet voice, Landon spoke at last. "When you go through with the marriage and quietly walk away from Cassandra without trouble, we'll amend our former agreement so you can become a Gage."

Emerson rose to his feet. "I'll need to get it in writing."

"Of course," Landon assured him.

"So do we arrange for them to meet?" Julian queried, rising, too, probably eager to leave to get his other business in order before his wedding and honeymoon.

"Do whatever the hell you want," Emerson snarled. "Just tell me when and where I get to meet my wife."

"So, it's done then," Landon concluded, still keeping

up his cool facade. But once Emerson stalked out of the conference room, Landon sighed wearily and scraped a hand along his face.

"Mother's going to throw a fit."

"Let's not tell her yet. He's not a Gage until he carries through…and he might fail," Jules said. Then he swung his full attention to Garrett. "So do you have something to tell us, bro?"

Garrett knew what he was referring to, of course.

It would have been hard for me to love anyone, when my whole life I've been in love with you.

She'd killed him with those words. He'd been replaying them in his head all night, dying in his bed, aroused and pained when he relived them. He wanted her by his side. He wanted every inch of her. Now, his chest swelled with emotion as he reached into his jacket pocket and pulled out a small blue velvet box. He opened it and extended it so that both his brothers could see the ring nestled at its center.

Julian chuckled and swung his head up with a look of incredulousness. "That ring is obscene, man. I've never seen anything as obscene in my life."

Garrett scowled at him. "Tiffany and Company doesn't do obscene."

"But *you* do."

Ignoring the jibe, Garrett studied the brilliant rock. It was the whitest, the purest and yes, the biggest he could find in seventy-six hours. An 8.39 carat, D, internally flawless round brilliant, in a solitaire platinum band. And he had every intention of putting it on Kate's ring finger.

"I need to make a statement," he murmured at Julian,

who seemed to be amused by the fact that Garrett had gotten himself in this mess in the first place.

"Statement. You mean like 'I'm a jerk and I had to make up for it with a big rock'?"

"Go to hell."

"Tsk, more respect, old man. You're marrying my fiancée's sister."

"If she'll have me," he grumbled.

"A little drastic of you to do this just so she doesn't move to Florida, don't you think?"

Garrett snorted.

He just wouldn't let her leave.

For years, he had seen that need in her, calling to him like a siren song. He had needed to summon more self-control every year not to cave in. He had prayed she would one day realize she was too good for him and move on. Now, he needed to prove to her the opposite. He needed to remind her what that night had meant to him, how it could have been between them all along if two deaths and a lot of regret hadn't stood between them.

He freaking *loved* her, too. More than anything or anyone.

He wasn't letting her go.

He was ready to chase her to Florida if he needed to.

He held the ring between his fingers and watched it catch the light. The man at the store said it was guaranteed to make a statement, and when Garrett had said, "Guaranteed to make her say yes?" he'd nodded amiably. If only the man knew half of it. That she could be pregnant with his child.

His stomach roiled once more at the thought, and he snapped the velvet Tiffany box closed.

If she wasn't pregnant, he couldn't wait for her to be.

She wanted a family. He hadn't realized how much he wanted one, too, until now.

He imagined being a father in eight months.

She didn't seem to want to consider the possibility, but he did. Hell, he even hoped she was pregnant. *Because she'd have to take me no matter what.*

It had been years since he'd had a father. Kate herself probably no longer remembered what her father had smelled like, felt like. Garrett barely remembered his own. But he could remember how good it had felt to have him around, and he burned with the desire to be one himself. Protective and just, but he wanted something their fathers hadn't given them.

He'd once thought he'd never marry. For Kate was out of his reach.

Now he would marry no one else. And he wanted a litter of little kids for them. Girls and boys.

He would bond with his boys over cars and planes, money and business....

As for girls, a picture of a red-haired little girl like Kate popped into his mind, and his toes almost curled with the love he already felt for that little thing he'd pamper like a princess.

Then he thought of Kate when she was young, the age when her father died. His chest constricted at the reminder. Garrett still dreamed about that night, and woke up drenched in sweat, hearing the sounds of gunshots. Sometimes in his dreams they were shooting at Kate and Molly. Sometimes at his brothers. And the worst part was that Garrett survived every time.

And somehow it was always Garrett's fault.

Would he never do things right? Would his actions always hurt the people he cared about?

He breathed out through his nose as he shoved the ring box into his suit pocket. It wasn't time yet. But it would be. And once he put that ring on her finger, it would never be undone. She would be his.

And he'd spend his life making things right for her. For them both.

Ten

Molly was freaking out in the bathroom of Eleanor Gage's master bedroom, waving her hands in front of her face as her cheeks turned crimson. "It's too tight, it's too tight. Kate, it's too tight."

"Molly, you just had it altered."

"Kate, I'm pregnant."

Kate's eyes widened with joy and disbelief. "You are? Molly!" Kate squealed and hugged her, and Molly crushed her in her arms. "Does Jules know?" Kate demanded.

"No! I'm saving it for tonight. I'm almost bursting with excitement and bursting out of this damn dress! I wish I'd just married him in my boho skirt. I know he'd love it because it's more me."

"Yes, but you've already bought this beautiful designer dress, and now we want you to wear it," Kate said, shushing her and trying to see where she could loosen the material to give her some air while Molly hyperventilated.

The dress had a lovely bell skirt and a tight top—very much like the bridesmaids' dresses that Kate and Beth wore, except the bridesmaids' dresses were blue.

"Molly, relax, you look stunning," Kate assured her. Molly nodded, and their gazes locked in the mirror. Kate's eyes began to tear up. "I love you, you know that?" Kate said softly, patting Molly's bun, which needed only the veil to be perfect.

Molly turned and squeezed Kate's hand, then placed it over her stomach—where she carried Julian's baby. "I want to beg you not to go, Kate. Especially now."

Kate could almost feel the connection between both their babies as she touched her sister's belly. Her throat constricted with the need to tell her sister she was pregnant, too. She imagined sharing all things pregnancy-related with Molly and her heart swelled. "I don't want to go, Molly. The thought of not seeing my niece or nephew and not being here for you…" *And of my child not being close to people who would offer so much love.* "I'm just afraid."

Sympathy flooded Molly's blue eyes. "Kate, I know… I know you don't want to see him, especially with him getting ready to marry someone else."

The reminder that the man she loved would marry someone else while she would be alone with his beautiful baby, somewhere else, set a new world of pain crashing down on her. Her eyes stung.

It might be her pregnancy hormones. Or the fact that time was galloping closer, ready to slam into her. It would be time to leave soon. It was time for her sister to marry. This morning Beth had told her she'd heard that Garrett had proposed to Cassandra already, and she'd wanted to warn Kate to be strong during the wedding in case he appeared with her.

He'd told her he wouldn't bring anyone. But if they were engaged, he'd bring her, of course.

Yes. Soon, it would be time for Garrett to let her know that it was done, that he was engaged to another woman. But then, she already knew from Beth.

She helped Molly with the veil, all the while blinking back the tears, and then she softly kissed her cheek. "You're the most beautiful bride I've ever seen."

"Kate, I want this for you," Molly said, gesturing at her wedding dress.

Kate nodded. "That's why I might just go after all, Moo. To find love and hopefully a family of my own."

They shared a forlorn smile, until Eleanor's shout from the bedroom snapped them out of it.

"It's time, my little Molly dear!"

Molly's eyes widened in excitement and she immediately puckered her lips into an O and drew in a series of little panting breaths that made Kate laugh. Poor Molly would probably be anxious for Julian to get her out of that dress tonight.

Molly smacked Kate's derriere. "Come on, sis. Let's go make that man mine," she said cheekily, and Kate adjusted her train around her arm and told her she'd be right out.

It was definitely the hormones. Or maybe a broken heart. Or the sentiment of watching her baby sister in a wedding gown.

Whatever it was, Kate sobbed quietly in the bathroom stall for a quick minute, and then wiped her tears and patted her makeup dry. Once her eyes didn't look so swollen, she went out into the gardens.

It was a perfect day for a wedding.

A breeze rustled through the oak trees. The sun blazed high in the sky, and it seemed the entire elite from Houston, Dallas, Austin and San Antonio was congregated at the Gage estate, all sumptuously dressed, many of the ladies wearing high-fashion hats on their heads.

Flowers framed the beautiful arched trellis, and the orchestra began softly with their violins while Kate quickly lined up behind Molly. She hadn't even thought she'd have the courage to see Garrett today, but he stood at the other end of the red-carpeted aisle next to Julian, whose smile was mesmerizing, his green eyes staring possessively at Molly.

Kate's gaze was magnetically drawn to Garrett, so stunning in his black tuxedo that her heart almost cracked with emotion when the "Bridal Chorus" began and Molly took the first step forward. Because this would never be her, walking up to him, like this.

Garrett's mouth was watering like crazy. He was supposed to watch Molly make her grand entrance but he could focus only on one redhead, and even from afar, he could see that Kate's eyes were full of tears, which just worried him and made him feel an insane need to go to her and embrace her and offer her support.

His thoughts filtered back to the day he'd met her. She and Molly had been brought up to the house by their father, the Gages' new bodyguard. Molly had been a little bitty thing, toddling over to give her lollipop to Julian. Kate had been just a tad older, but she'd been as open and chatty as a teenager, immediately warming up to his mother, asking why this? Why that?

She'd made him scowl, and when she'd turned to talk to Julian and warn him not to take Molly's lollipop, Garrett had immediately wanted her to pay attention to him, too. It had been the story of his life. Wanting her attention, her eyes on him, wanting everything from her and hating that he wanted it. He'd wanted to be the apple of her eye, and instead, he'd been the idiot who took away her father.

He'd promised himself he'd be her hero, and he'd tried like hell to protect her from everything he could—especially himself. When all he'd wanted was her. He'd withdrawn with ruthless self-discipline, telling himself that he'd never deserve Kate like Julian deserved Molly.

Today Garrett's eyes were wide open. True, the past was loaded with regrets, but when he thought of the future, one without Kate at the center of it was unfathomable. No man on this earth would ever love and care for Kate and fight for her happiness more than Garrett would. Chest bursting with emotion, he watched the woman he loved walk behind her sister. He saw how her soft smile trembled with emotion, and God, he wanted to hug her and kiss those tears away, telling her whatever changed in her life, he'd always be her constant.

He couldn't take his eyes off her as she came up the aisle. He imagined her walking up to him and his heart stuttered in his chest, he loved her so much.

Now she took her place across from Garrett as her sister tied the knot with the love of her life, and all Garrett knew was that he wanted to do this with Kate. He'd have Kate. Or he'd have no one.

"Dearly beloved, we are gathered here today..." The

priest began the ceremony, and for several minutes, Garrett waited for Kate's gaze to turn to him. Finally, her eyes flicked over to his, and his gut seized with need. She looked so beautiful. Her lips shone in a coral color, her blue eyes highlighted by the sapphire fabric of her dress. A silent plea brimmed in the depths of those eyes, and whatever it was she wanted, Garrett wanted to give it to her.

Not because he'd promised her father that he would. But because he was selfish and he got high on her smiles, got completely drugged and deliciously drunk with her happiness.

"I, Molly, take you, Julian John, to be my husband…"

As soon as he heard Molly speak, Garrett imagined Kate speaking that same vow to him. His chest squeezed as their gazes held across the altar, Kate's blue eyes continuing to tear him to pieces.

She still wanted to leave, didn't she?

But he wouldn't let her.

Not after he'd had her trembling in his arms and whispering his name and giving him everything he'd always wanted.

He'd told himself every night for the past thirty nights that she might have felt pity for him, or that they were just a man and a woman in bed together, getting caught in the moment. It was bull. What they'd been caught up in had been years and years of denied attraction. Burning chemistry. Heated glances. And he was sick and tired of denying himself *her.*

The day she'd made love to him had been the best day of his existence. And he wanted to have her in his arms, where she belonged, every day and night in his future.

"You may now kiss the bride!"

Kate blinked and tore her eyes from his, looking startled as Julian grabbed Molly and twirled her around.

"Oh, crap!"

They ended up tangled in the train, and Kate came instantly to the rescue. Kate. Always taking care of Molly.

"I got it," she said, laughing as she detached the train and Julian proceeded to carry a laughing Molly away, the blaring sound of the "Wedding March" following them.

Watching Kate struggle, Garrett stalked down the aisle, grabbed the other end of the tulle fabric and brought it over, watching her duck her head to avoid his gaze.

"Thanks," she said, and he wanted to kiss her. God, why was this so difficult? They'd grown up together. She was the only woman who knew him, truly knew him. What he liked and loathed. That he would never truly feel like he deserved a life of his own.

If he was going to open up with someone, it should be easy to do it with her.

But the way she was acting skittish and defensive filled him with dread. And he knew that this was going to be one of the hardest things he'd ever done.

She struggled with the tulle. When he reached out and captured her small hands, she sucked in an audible breath. His heart pounded as she looked up at him, those blue eyes wide and concerned.

"Tell me if I'm mistaken—" his voice was low "—but did my brother just marry your sister?"

She didn't smile, but looked intently into his eyes as if she was as entranced as he was. "It only took a full hour, Garrett. You couldn't have missed it," she said.

Her mouth, the way it moved, drove him insane. "Apparently I did."

"You were standing right there. Where were you? Mars?" She straightened and rolled her eyes as she started walking away, the tulle clutched against her chest, and he had to raise his voice a bit to be heard.

"I was in my bedroom, Kate. With you in my arms."

She went utterly still, her back to him, and he knew she remembered. He could feel it in the air, burning between them.

But she didn't turn. Instead, she started down the path that led to the Gage mansion. Garrett fell into step beside her.

"Kay, I need to talk to you," he said.

"If it's to tell me about your wedding, I already know. Congratulations," she said.

He cocked a brow. "Then maybe you can tell me the details, since apparently you know more about it than I do? Dammit, I need to talk to you somewhere *private*."

He grabbed her elbow to halt her, but she immediately yanked it free. "I need to talk to you, too, but I'm not doing it here. Nor am I doing it *today*."

Simmering with frustration, he followed her again,. "Well, I *am*. So just listen to me."

Stopping her, he forced her to turn and gazed into those accusing blue eyes, trying to find the words to begin the wrenching of his damned black soul. "I don't know what happened to me the other day, Katie....What you told me left me so damn winded, I swear I didn't know where to begin...."

Her hands flew to her ears. "Not here, please, *please, not here!*"

He pulled her arms down, scowling. "I know I hurt you, I know you don't want me to apologize, but I need to say I am sorry. I am sorry for how things have gone down and for hurting you. I'm sorry for how it happened, Katie. I wish I'd done it differently. If I could take it back, I would, if only to get you to stop looking at me like you are just now."

She whipped around to face him, her eyes flashing in fury. "You wish to take the night back, that's what you wish? Oh, you're something special, do you know that? You're something else. I can't even believe I let you put your filthy paws on me, you no-good—"

"Goddamn it, I really didn't want to do it this way, Kay. But you're giving me no choice!" Jaw clamped, he grabbed her and swept her into his arms and stalked across the gardens toward the house.

"Wha—" The tulle train fell inch by inch from her grasp and trailed a path behind them as she kicked and squirmed and hit his chest. "Garrett, stop! Put me down! What are you *doing?*"

He kicked the front doors open and carried her up the stairs, his jaw like steel, his hands blatantly gripping her buttocks. "Something I should've done a long, long time ago."

Kate froze for a second, and then struggled with more effort. "Put me down!" she screeched.

He squeezed her bottom as he charged down the hall and into his old bedroom, kicking the door shut behind him. "I'm not apologizing for the night I made love to you. Dammit, Kate, I'm apologizing for being responsible for your father's *death!*"

He put her down on the bench at the foot of his old bed and stepped back so she didn't kick him in the groin.

She went utterly still, but her chest heaved up and down, and damned if that wasn't an attractive sight.

He expelled a long breath and continued. "Kate, I'm not going to apologize for the time you were mine. I won't. I apologized once, but I didn't mean it. I don't regret a second of that time with you. Except not being more careful with you and more than anything, for not doing it sooner."

She sat there, stunned and panting, and Garrett was only just beginning. His necktie was almost choking him as all his emotions surfaced like a hurricane gathering force.

"I apologize for not listening to your father that night, Kate. For being stupid and not listening—"

"Don't!" she pleaded, raising her palms. "Garrett, please don't apologize for that. Or for anything. Please stop apologizing to me. It was an accident. And it was his duty. My father would have…gladly died for you, for any Gage, for any reason. He was passionate about his job, and he was as passionate about you boys as if you were his children. He'd have done it over and over for you, Garrett. He loved you and I love you. I've always loved you."

Her words were like a salve. They might never absolve him, but they appeased him, tamed the dark regret inside him. And stoked the little flickering flame of new hope there.

"You do love me, don't you, Freckles?"

She met his gaze in silence. My God, *her face.* The blush spread everywhere, it seemed, and Garrett trembled with the urge to undress her and see that flush crawl along her skin.

When she didn't say a word, neither affirming nor denying it, he knelt.

* * *

Kate's eyes almost popped out of their sockets as Garrett Gage knelt at her feet.

"You asked me what I wanted from you—Kate, I want everything. The works. Yes, I want kids, I want to be your husband. I know I robbed you of a real family, and I want to give you one. I want to be the father of your children…not because I promised I would take care of you. Because I'm crazy-sick in love with you."

His words sucked the wind out of her.

She sat there, clutching her stomach, not even remembering where the tulle had ended up falling on their way here. Runaway tears streamed down her cheeks as the things Molly and Beth had told her about a Clarks-Gage wedding vanished from her head and she realized with a fluttering heart that Garrett Gage was proposing to her.

"Kate, I've never felt like this before. I can't think clearly when it comes to you. I've been trying to make you stay and at the same time that has driven you away. Don't go, baby. Stay with me. Here. Be my wife. Let me love you like you deserve."

She cried even harder, not believing this was happening. She had dreamed about this. For years. To the point that now her entire life and all her decisions revolved around forgetting it. Around trying not to want what she could *never* have.

And now Garrett Gage knelt, dark and beautiful at her feet, his face somber in its intensity, his gaze like liquid fire.

"If you think this has to do with the promise I made to your father, it doesn't," he murmured as he took her smaller hand within both of his. "I made that promise a long time ago and I've tried to keep it as best as I could.

No, this is about me wanting to promise you, the woman I love, my future."

She wiped her eyes, and squeezed one of his hands with hers. "What about C-Cassandra...?"

"She's marrying Emerson. Our half brother."

"Wh-what do you mean h-half—?"

A movement in the doorway made them both look up in surprise.

"Kate! What...?" Beth blinked. "I'm sorry...uh. This is a bad time, isn't it?"

Garrett nodded, but Kate shook her head and wiped the rest of her tears away. "What is it, Beth?"

Beth pointed in the direction of the stairs behind her. "They're all seated at the tables. And the maid of honor and best man need to speak before the toast."

Garrett dropped his head and cursed under his breath.

"We'll be right there, Beth," Kate said, trembling from head to toe as she rose to her feet.

Garrett held her up and stroked his thumb along her jawline. "You can answer me later," he said softly.

She nodded and rushed to the bathroom to pat her face dry with a tissue, making sure her mascara wasn't dripping all over her face. Garrett waited outside in the hall for her, and every cell in her body screamed at her to fling herself into his arms when she realized he was still there. But she didn't.

In silence, they went downstairs and into the gardens, and halfway there, after the backs of their hands bumped several times, he took her hand within his and led her across to their table.

Her throat closed, and she tried very hard not to think about the gesture and how many times she'd wanted it. It screamed "boyfriend" in her mind. Lover. Love.

Feeling as though five hundred pairs of eyes were on them as they made their way through the tables to the far end of the room, Kate held her gaze on the bride and groom.

Her fingers tingled when her hand unlatched from Garrett's and they each headed to their places on opposite sides of the long table, where Molly and Julian sat watching them with wide smiles. Garrett went to stand at Julian's side, and Kate stood next to Molly. Eleanor had indicated that she didn't want to speak, and she seemed to be hiding behind a tissue right now, but Kate remembered how the groom's mother always thought it proper that ladies go first. So Kate was the first to speak.

Regrettably.

She cleared her throat several times and shakily grabbed a small microphone, struggling to keep her voice level as she tried to quiet her racing mind. "Molly had a favorite story she liked for me to read," she said into the microphone, keeping her eyes on Molly to keep herself focused. "There was a part she loved to hear, when Piglet asked Winnie the Pooh, 'How do you spell love?' And Pooh answered 'You don't spell it.... You feel it.'"

She blinked back her tears as she studied the delightful little bundle by the name of Molly, the only blood family Kate had known for over two decades. Seeing her sister so happy as she started a family of her own with Julian, while Kate herself had a baby in her tummy from the man she loved and a proposal she had always dreamed of, made her suddenly feel weightless with joy. Laughing to herself, she lifted her glass with her free hand.

"Molly and Julian, you guys felt that love for each

other before you could spell it. And I'm just glad you didn't listen to me, Moo, when I filled your head with warnings and my own fears. I'm glad you listened to your heart."

People clapped and drank, and Kate sat down only to hear Garrett's sexy voice coming through the microphone next. "For the better part of my life I've thought it my duty to protect Molly from your claws, little bro."

Julian threw back his head and let out a great peal of laughter, soon joined by all the other guests, and Garrett winked at Molly. "I got to be the ogre separating you two for years, for which I hope you won't always hate me, Molly."

"I forgive you if you finally kiss my sister!" Molly shot back, throwing him a white rose she'd plucked from the centerpiece.

Garrett caught it and laughed, then glanced at Kate and held it in the air, as if promising to give it to her. Tucking it into his pocket, he glanced back at the groom.

"There's no denying that I got to be the voice of reason when Kate and Molly came into our lives, Jules. Because I knew better than you that we were both done for."

He turned his attention to his new sister-in-law next. "Molly, my brother loves you more than anything in the world," he told her, lifting his glass now. "And if you take care of my brother, I promise I will not only kiss your sister, but I will not rest until I make her my wife."

The guests whooped and cheered, as Julian stood to slap him on the back and everyone seemed to glance at Kate for a moment. Their smiles almost pleaded with her not to be stupid and just snatch up this man for herself.

And she would.

Of course she would.

She knew Garrett would want an answer, but before she could give him anything, he would need to know that she was pregnant.

Oh, God. She was having his child, and he loved her. He. Loved. Her.

The hours sped by. Soon, they were served the artichoke hearts with a special tangy mustard sauce, a variety of meats, an assortment of vegetables and desserts to spare.

By the time Molly and Julian were ready for the first dance, Garrett made his way to Kate, and she rose to her feet, anticipation making her heart race. She didn't know if she could postpone her answer until she had a chance to talk to him about the pregnancy. There was impatience etched across his features, as though he'd been waiting too long already to hear her acceptance and he wouldn't wait anymore.

He would want an answer now—she could see it in his eyes. Eyes that wouldn't stop staring at her.

Garrett's heart crashed into his rib cage as he approached Kate, who looked so warm and inviting as she waited for him to get close.

He let his gaze drift down her body, taking in the perky breasts encased in that corset dress he'd seen her try on, the form-fitting fabric that hugged her shapely hips and the skirt that flared over her legs. She wore her hair loose. Long and wavy and so damned glossy it looked like satin, it tumbled past her shoulders. Feather earrings clung to her little ears. And her eyes…

When he looked up at her eyes and found them staring at him with shy vulnerability, he almost couldn't take it, he wanted her so much.

He wanted these people gone, wanted her intimately, in his arms.

"Dance with me," he said quietly as he gently pulled her into his arms. She hooked her arms underneath his, and her hands curved over his shoulders from behind as she pressed her body to him and tucked her face under his chin.

He closed his eyes and savored the feel of her as she drew an invisible pattern with her fingertips along his back. She moved fluidly against him, like she belonged in his arms.

His insides thrummed with impatience as he held one arm around her waist, then slowly reached into his jacket pocket and pulled out the velvet Tiffany box. He clasped her left hand and slid the ring onto her finger, then lifted her hand so that she noticed the jewel as he kissed her knuckles, one by one.

He'd never been so impatient in his life.

He couldn't understand how he'd waited to claim her for so long, for he couldn't handle another second of wondering if she was still planning to move somewhere else.

"I need to hear you say yes," he murmured, tucking her hand under his arm as he kissed her ear softly. Her hair caressed her shoulders as she angled her head backwards an inch or two, and she looked at him with those blue eyes, shining with tears and emotion.

I love you, she'd said.

He was burning to hear it again.

"Say it, Kate," he pressed her, cupping the back of her head in one hand. Impatiently he fitted his lips to hers and hungrily searched inside her mouth for her response. When her tongue pushed back thirstily against him, she set him on fire. He splayed his hand at the small of her back and pressed her tightly to him as he dragged his mouth up to her ear. "Tell me yes."

She grabbed his jaw and turned his head so she could whisper, "I need to tell you something first."

He groaned, already burning with desire, needing to be with her. "Tell me after you've said yes."

She smiled. "You'd take me anyway? Whatever I have to say?"

He shot her a solemn gaze. "Yes, Kate. I would. Tell me yes, and then tell me what you want to say to me."

"Yes, I'll marry you. We're having a baby."

He drew back, staring wordlessly. His astonishment was so complete, his disbelief so overwhelming, he wasn't even breathing. "What baby?"

"Our baby, Garrett. We're having a baby."

"You're pregnant," he said, as if in a daze.

She bit her lower lip, her eyes shining with wariness and excitement and concern.

He shook his head to clear it, but it was full of one thought. Baby. Father. Parents. *She'll give me a child.... She loves me.... She'll give me a baby....*

"Kate...when were you going to tell me this? When?"

"I'm telling you now."

"And you were still going to Florida *without me?*"

Kate wiped away her tears.

"Were you?" he demanded.

"No," she admitted. "I'm not going anywhere. This is my home."

He was shocked. Suddenly he bent and kissed her stomach. "You're not joking me?"

"No. Molly's pregnant, too, but don't say anything."

He straightened again and seized her by the shoulders. "Holy hell, you have to say yes now."

"It was yes before, Garrett. It's…always yes. I've dreamed this. I've wanted it for so long."

He was reeling.

He looked at her and felt that same hot punch to his solar plexus. Then he pulled her back against him, infinitely closer.

He raised a languid hand to stroke the shell of her ear with the back of one curled finger. "Kate…" he murmured adoringly.

She gave him a smile, her eyes glowing. "Yes, Garrett?"

Jamming his fingers into her hair, he tipped her head back so she held his gaze. "God, we've wasted so much time, Kate."

"You said you weren't afraid. To love somebody." She cupped his jaw. "I am. I *was*. I won't be anymore. I'm going to love you like crazy if you let me."

"I'll not only let you, I'll encourage you. I'll do anything possible to make it true." He stroked her belly with one hand, and her scalp with the other. "Have you gone to the doctor?"

"I was going to. I kept hoping Beth and Molly were wrong. That you wouldn't marry Cassandra. And maybe… I'd try one more time to make you love me. Be honest with you this time. No more sneaky tactics to get your attention."

"Kate, you couldn't be sneaky if you tried."

"Garrett, I didn't want to trap you into marriage, please know that."

"I know, Freckles. You don't need to tell me this. But didn't you know? You trapped me with these ages ago…."

He stroked her seven freckles that he adored, then let his finger drift down to the flesh of her lips. "Trapped. Caught. I hardly ever got to chase you and I know you wanted me to."

"I didn't."

"You did."

"All right then, I did." She started running across the gardens, and for a stunned moment, he didn't realize she was heading back to the bedroom where he'd just proposed. Then everything in him burst to action and he chased after her.

Eleven

Garrett drove them over to his apartment, and their excitement made the air crackle between them.

She loved how he'd chased her, and caught her. The crazy man had *tickled* her. They'd danced together, laughed, enjoyed each other. Kate had never felt so free or happy. Garrett had never looked so content, his face never faltering from the dazzling white smile that curled her toes and warmed her tummy.

Now he led her down the hall of his apartment, and her body was going crazy from wanting him.

Their footsteps were rushed as she tried unfastening her dress and Garrett tossed his tux jacket on the floor, then left a trail of clothing to his room—bowtie, shoes, socks, vest.

"I can't wait," he said as he jerked off his snowy-white shirt.

Kate was breathing in little pants at the sight of him bare-chested. He watched her struggle to unlace her dress from the back for a moment, then said, "Turn around, let me get that."

His voice was gruff with desire, and her legs trembled as he got her dress undone. He eased the top half of her dress down to her waist, and then she caught her breath when his thumbs caressed her back in slow circles. She shuddered when he set a kiss at the nape of her neck as he started easing the dress off her hips, then splayed his hands over her rib cage and pressed her back against him before turning her around.

She wasn't wearing a bra and she mewed softly when his hands covered her aching breasts. Then she tilted her face upward as his mouth searched for and found hers.

He teased her with his tongue and rubbed her nipples with his thumbs. His body rocked against her, and Kate couldn't stand the agony.

"Garrett…"

All her emotions had spun and churned for days and weeks, and now she needed him inside her.

With her dress pooled at her ankles, he caressed his hands along the sides of her stockinged thighs. "Do you want me?" His low, erotically textured voice drove her insane.

"So much," she gasped, pushing against him so she could feel how much he wanted her, the proof in the erection straining against his dress slacks.

"Do you love me?" He palmed her between her legs, where a pool of heat had already gathered at the apex.

"Like nothing in my life."

He squeezed her sex in his palm. "I love you, Kate." He dragged his tongue along her neck and down her shoulders as he hooked his fingers around the waistband of her stockings and tugged off the clinging material. He urged her onto the bench at the end of the bed as he removed them, and she sat and watched his dark head as he bent to tongue a wet path down her bare legs. Tingles of pleasure raced through her body. He tossed the stockings aside, and Kate edged back onto the bed, tossing away some of the decorative pillows as he unfastened his slacks and got naked.

He was beautifully masculine, tanned and hard, and swollen with desire for her.

"The last time I was with you has haunted me," he whispered as he started lowering his body over hers, his arm muscles flexing. Swallowing with a little sound of need, she spread her thighs to welcome him and he settled between them, his urgency matching hers as their tongues tangled heatedly.

"I haven't stopped thinking about it for a second, either," she admitted, nipping his mouth, then kissing his jaw, anxious to claim him like he was claiming her.

He teased her breasts with his thumbs, then grazed the straining peaks with his teeth. She moaned, and he lapped her with his tongue to make her delirious.

"You like that, Freckles? You like my mouth all over you?"

"I love everything you do to me."

He chuckled softly, his breath bathing her nipple tips as he mouthed her breasts, alternating from one to the other. He caressed them until she couldn't wait and was pumping her body eagerly for his penetration.

He primed her with one finger, then two. "I'll be careful with you," he vowed, and kissed her lips. "And you." He kissed her stomach, and Kate's heart unwound like a ribbon when she realized he was talking to their unborn child. “Freckles, I wanted this. You. I wanted something of ours.”

“Then make me yours,” she whispered.

He gripped her hips and meshed his mouth to hers as he entered her. She arched up for his thrust, clutching him. “Garrett.”

He grabbed the sides of her thighs and kept them slightly raised as he inched deeper into her body. She tossed her head back with a grimace of pain that became absolute, exquisite pleasure when he was fully inside.

She was so turned on that every time he pulled out, her sex muscles clung to him, preventing him from leaving her. She wanted more of him, all of him, inside her.

She cried out when he started thrusting harder and deeper, and an explosion of colors rushed through her mind, stretching her nerve endings until they snapped and released. He growled and strained above her, and they rode out the pleasure together.

“That was amazing,” she gasped when Garrett rolled over to the side and pulled her up against him. “You’re so amazing.” She hugged him, and he returned her hug, his arms hot and tight around her.

He clasped the back of her head and stared meaningfully into her eyes. “Every night from now on I want you sleeping in my arms.”

“I’m not complaining.”

He adjusted her against him so that he was embracing her from behind and his hands were splayed on her stomach. He spoke close to her temple. “If he’s a boy, we’ll name him after our fathers. Jonathan David Gage. And a girl…you’ll drive me crazy if you give me a girl.”

“You’re the one giving it to me,” she laughingly answered, and he turned her face by the chin and brushed her freckles with his lips.

"Always so contrary, my Kate."

"Garrett? Pinch me." He pinched her bottom, and she squealed.

He chuckled, clearly liking it. "Ask me to pinch you again."

"One's enough. I'm convinced I'm not dreaming now."

"You have a lovely bottom. If you let me pinch it again, I'll kiss it afterward."

She laughed. Feeling little tingles in her body, she nodded, and she felt the pinch that made her squeak, and then she felt his kiss, with tongue. It made her moan softly and cuddle back to him, wondering when she could have him again.

"Convinced it's no dream?" he murmured, brushing her hair behind her forehead.

With a smile that almost hurt, she turned over and pressed her face into his chest and stroked her fingers absently across his nipples, growing thoughtful. "Now what was it you were saying about a half brother?"

"You'll meet him soon," he told her. "He looks like me, actually."

"Wow, that good?"

He laughed. "Don't even think about staring for a moment longer than necessary."

"Why would I when I have you?" She tucked her head under his chin. "Why didn't we know about him?"

"Mother didn't want to know about him. But I think it's time we set the past behind us, don't you, Kate?"

"Yes, Garrett. I agree wholeheartedly."

Twelve

Sitting on her front stoop, Kate spotted Garrett's silver Audi turning around the corner and her smile widened. As soon as thc car camc to a stop, shc started for the passenger door.

He couldn't even get out, she got in so fast. "Hey," she said.

His car smelled of him, of leather and spices, deliciously male, and it almost made her dizzy.

"Hey." He reached out and squeezed her hand, bending over and kissing her lips softly. "You look good."

She smiled. "So do you."

Once they arrived at the clinic, Kate filled out the paperwork while Garrett sat, enormous in the little chair out in the waiting room, pulling and pulling at his tie. There were pictures of babies and pregnant women hanging on the walls, but he only had eyes for Kate as she walked back toward him.

Soon, they were led inside to the ultrasound room.

Kate was lying down patiently as the doctor came inside, greeted them and pulled up her robe. After the doctor smeared a cold gel on her stomach, a little blob appeared on the screen.

Garrett had been standing back, but now he approached, his eyes on the screen.

"There we go," Dr. Lowry said.

Garrett peered at the screen, and Kate reached for his hand and squeezed, suddenly extremely excited. He squeezed back even harder, and smiled down at the screen.

"That noise you hear is the heartbeat," the doctor explained.

They were both silent as they registered this. Then the doctor took some measurements, and estimated the date of conception to be…of course, the night she accosted Garrett in his bedroom when he was sick.

"Thank God for strep," he said to himself, and his eyes glittered when he looked at her, as though that was the best thing that could have ever happened to him.

Sharing this with him was incredible. Irrevocable. She could feel the connection as they watched their child on that screen together.

The doctor gave them the estimated delivery date. "So we will be seeing you in two months to find out what you're having."

"Do we really want to know?" Kate asked Garrett.

"Hell, yes, we do."

She smiled and nodded.

The doctor slapped the folder shut. "In the meantime, everything looks fine, Mr. and Mrs. Devaney. You have yourselves a good rest of the day."

"It's *Gage*."

The doctor turned to Garrett. "Oh?" He quickly checked his folder, flustered and confused.

"I filled my name in as Devaney," Kate whispered to Garrett as she wiped the gel off her stomach. His eyes homed in on her bare skin like he wanted to lick the gel up and bury his face in her belly button.

"You're a Gage, too, starting tomorrow," he said flatly.

She rolled her eyes. "Of course I am. I just felt odd using the name before we go to city hall and church."

He helped her down from the examining table and kissed her softly but quickly. "You've always been a Gage, Kate. You've been mine from the start. I didn't need to sleep with you to show you that."

"Maybe you did." She smirked, patting her stomach, and he laughed.

Outside the clinic, he pulled her up against him when they got to his car. "Thank you, Freckles."

"For what?"

"For that night you spent in my arms," he whispered, framing her face in his hands and kissing her. "For agreeing to spend a lifetime of nights with me."

"No, Garrett," she said, cupping his face right back. "Thank *you* for asking."

* * * * *

If you liked Kate's story, don't miss these other novels from Red Garnier:

THE SECRETARY'S BOSSMAN BARGAIN
PAPER MARRIAGE PROPOSITION
WRONG MAN, RIGHT KISS

All available now, from Harlequin Desire!

#2299 YOUR RANCH...OR MINE?

The Good, the Bad and the Texan • by Kathie DeNosky

Five-card draw suddenly becomes a game of hearts when professional poker player Lane Donaldson wins half a Texas ranch and discovers he's soon to be housemates with the spirited beauty who inherited the other half!

#2300 FROM SINGLE MOM TO SECRET HEIRESS

Dynasties: The Lassiters • by Kristi Gold

High-rolling lawyer Logan Whittaker tracks down a secret heiress, only to find a feisty single mom who isn't necessarily ready to join the scandal-plagued Lassiter family. But what if Hannah's real home is with him?

#2301 THE SARANTOS BABY BARGAIN

Billionaires and Babies • by Olivia Gates

Now guardian to an orphaned little girl, Andreas Sarantos wants only the best for her, which means marrying the baby's adoptive mother—his ex-wife. But their arrangement becomes less than convenient when his passion for Naomi reignites....

#2302 CAROSELLI'S ACCIDENTAL HEIR

The Caroselli Inheritance • by Michelle Celmer

Forced to marry and produce an heir, Antonio Caroselli is about to say "I do" when his ex shows up—pregnant! He's always wanted Lucy, but will she believe in their love after she finds out about the terms of the will?

#2303 THE LAST COWBOY STANDING

Colorado Cattle Barons • by Barbara Dunlop

After a disastrous first meeting, Colorado rancher Travis and city-gal Danielle don't expect to cross paths again. But when they end up in a Vegas hotel suite together, there's no denying the depths of their desires.

#2304 A MERGER BY MARRIAGE

Las Vegas Nights • by Cat Schield

When spunky hotel executive Violet Fontaine inherits a rival company's stock, she helps the enigmatic JT Stone reclaim control of his family's company the only way she can—by marrying him!

Turn the page for a sneak peek at

Kristi Gold's

FROM SINGLE MOM TO SECRET HEIRESS,

the second novel in Harlequin® Desire's

***DYNASTIES: THE LASSITERS** series.*

The Lassiter family lawyer has some surprise news for one stunning woman...

She looked prettier than a painted picture come to life. Yep. Trouble with a capital *T* if he didn't get his mind back on business.

"After you learn the details of your share of the Lassiter fortune, you'll be able to buy me dinner next time." *Next time?* Man, he was getting way ahead of himself, and that was totally out of character for his normally cautious self.

Hannah looked about as surprised as he felt over the comment. "That all depends on if I actually agree to accept my share, and that's doubtful."

He couldn't fathom anyone in their right mind turning down that much money. But before he had a chance to toss out an opinion, their waiter showed up with their entrées.

Logan ate his food with the gusto of a field hand, while Hannah basically picked at hers, the same way she had with the salad. By the time they were finished, and the plates were cleared, he had half a mind to invite her into the nearby bar to discuss business. But dark and cozy wouldn't help rein in his libido.

HDEXP0414

Hannah tossed her napkin aside and folded her hands before her. "Okay, we've put this off long enough. Tell me the details."

Logan took a drink of water in an attempt to rid the dryness in his throat. "The funds are currently in an annuity. You have the option to leave it as is and take payments. Or you can claim the lump sum. Your choice."

"How much?" she said after a few moments.

He noticed she looked a little flushed and decided retiring to the bar might not be a bad idea after all. "Maybc wc should go into the lounge so you can have a drink before I continue."

Frustration showed in her expression. "I don't need a drink."

He'd begun to think he might. "Just a glass of wine to take the edge off."

She leaned forward and nailed him with a glare. *"How much?"*

"Five million dollars."

"I believe I will have that drink now."

Desire